ALL HIS LOVE FOR
Christmas

The story of rescue...

The story of love...

The story of FURever

de de Cox

Copyright © 2020 by de de Cox

All His Love for Christmas

All rights reserved. No part of this publication may be reproduced, distributed, or transmitted in any form or by any means, including photocopying, recording, or other electronic or mechanical methods, without the prior written permission of the publisher, except in the case of brief quotations embodied in critical reviews and certain other noncommercial uses permitted by copyright law. For permission requests, write to the publisher, addressed "Attention: Permissions Coordinator," at info@beyondpublishing.net

Quantity sales special discounts are available on quantity purchases by corporations, associations, and others. For details, contact the publisher at the address above.

Orders by U.S. trade bookstores and wholesalers. Email info@BeyondPublishing.net

CREDITS

Photography and Production:	Austin Ozier / Ozier Productions
HMUA:	Scooter Minyard
Asst to HMUA:	Jeanette Moore
Male Model:	Bo Cox
Female Model:	Sky Jackson
Location:	The Minyard Family Home, Louisville, KY
Inspiration:	Pat Gary
Contributor:	Robyn Thomas

The Beyond Publishing Speakers Bureau can bring authors to your live event. For more information or to book an event contact the Beyond Publishing Speakers Bureau speak@BeyondPublishing.net

The Author can be reached directly at *KentuckyRomanceAuthor.com*

Manufactured and printed in the United States of America distributed globally by BeyondPublishing.net

New York | Los Angeles | London | Sydney

ISBN: 978-1-952884-13-9

DEDICATION

Growing up on a small farm in Rooster Run, Kentucky, we were surrounded by animals. Cats, dogs, horses, pigs, chickens – all ran the farm. So many FURbabies to love on and to return the love unconditionally. When I decided to write this book to lead into the RESCUE ME series, I had no idea how GOD would open the doors to rescue. You do realize GOD loves animals, too.

I met Bebe through my HMUA, Scooter Minyard, and his assistant, Jeanette Moore. A beautiful little white Chihuahua who loved to be held. She was a trooper the entire day of the photoshoot. All rescues have a story for that is how they become rescued. I watched as Scooter held Bebe. Folk say you can see a person's soul by looking into their eyes. Scooter's soul is pure and kind. The love given to an animal is like no other. For in this special kind of love is where we hide our feelings and our emotions. Our FURbabies will never hurt us. They may lick us to death. They keep our innermost secrets. The bond of rescue can never be destroyed. It remains as a constant to remind us of what giving truly is about. For one special day, I was able to see through Bebe's eyes what Scooter and Nayandy give so freely – adoration and love.

My family is also part of rescue. When you follow me, you will see that our family has three: Elizabeth and Rocky (our bulldogs) and Sunny (our cat). All three rescues. All three loved and spoiled, as all FURbabies should be.

As an animal lover, I adore all the groups that showcase our FURbabies. One in particular caught my attention. It was the "OFFICIAL BULLDOGS ARE AWESOME CLUB" site. On this site are some of the most amazing and hysterical stories of bullies that you will ever read. I started paying close attention to Gertie The Bulldog's Deep

Thoughts posts. There was never a moment when I was not smiling at some of the predicaments that Gertie would get into or the fact that she was a TRUE DIVA, a TRUE QUEEN. Daily, Gertie would share her thoughts on nutrition, exercise, health, and how demanding life was being a Queen. Gertie's only passion and true love were sprinkled donuts. She would comment on how everyone needed sprinkles in their life.

Gertie's owners, Steven and Gloria Rabinowitz, are the real deal. You knew by reading the daily inspirations that Gertie was rotten and she ruled their home. Unexpectedly, Gertie crossed over the rainbow bridge. The entire bulldog community was devastated. Anyone with an animal knows that when we lose our FURbaby, our entire world stops. We have lost a piece of our heart. A piece of our existence for getting up in the morning and stepping in slobber. A piece of our heart for those moments when they don't want to go out in the rain and you pick up an umbrella to be sure they do not get wet – doesn't matter about you and if you catch pneumonia. We all hurt for those who lose their FURbabies. This story of love is for Gertie, the Rabinowitz family and our club. Gertie was born July 4, 2009 and crossed August 4, 2020.

And so I dedicate this last book in the Two Degrees Series – ALL HIS LOVE FOR CHRISTMAS (the story of rescue…the story of love…the story of FURever) to Rocky, Elizabeth, Sunny, Bebe and Gertie (and their mommas and daddies).

ALL HIS LOVE FOR
Christmas

"I never asked for your help!" "You did", Harper exclaimed. "You asked for my help while lying there upside down in your car. Don't tell me you did not need to be rescued," Harper stated in her matter of fact voice to Crispin. She was seething. Who did he think he was? Every woman in town was pining for him. Harper saw nothing special that would be of interest to her. In the few short weeks that Crispin had returned home for the holidays, all Harper had heard was "did you know that Dr. Steele was back in town?" Harper wanted to tell the world that yes, she knew "Dr." Steele was in town. She was the one who rescued him and brought him home.

Crispin watched the emotions flood Harper's face. Before Harper could utter the next word, Crispin pulled her close to him. "You need this more than me," Crispin told her. And before Harper could ask what did she need, Crispin placed his hand on the back of Harper's neck and pulled her in to his lips. Harper could not breathe. She did not want nor desire Dr. Steele's affectionate displays in public but Harper could not stop her lips from betraying her. The kiss grew intent with sexual innuendo. Harper did not want him to stop. She inhaled to catch her breath.

Crispin stepped back. "There will be more of that. Trust me. You can tell me how much you despise me, but actions speak louder than words. I promise it will happen again and I always keep my promise." Harper took the back of her hand and wiped the kiss off her lips in a dramatic fashion. Crispin laughed and rubbed his thumb across her lips swollen with desire. Harper muttered under her breath "never".

INTRO

Harper could not believe that she had still not made it back to the shelter with all three of the little convicts that she had rescued earlier that morning. The snow falling was preventing a good travel time. Harper could tell from the whining in the back seat that a quick stop was going to be needed in order to continue the journey. So she did what she had done so many times on her way back to the office – she pulled over to the side of the road. Praying, that she would be able to get back on the road due to the snowdrifts and ruts she had encountered.

Lawd, they were taking their sweet time. What in the world was holding their attention? Harper had reached into the van to grab some treats to entice them to return. She was cold. If she was cold, they had to be cold. Harper heard their barking. This was not the typical play bark. This was a bark of concern. Harper began the walk to where their barking was echoing. Something was not right. The hair on her arms began to rise like needles. Harper knew she was going to have to walk to where the incessant barking was taking place. Her heart was racing as she began the track through the snow covered road. Harper was hoping against hope she was not going to find what she already knew was there. The car tracks disappeared. Harper halted. She heard their whine. They had discovered something or someone. She peered down into the dip of the land and there IT was. A car was turned upside down. Harper did the only thing she knew. She sat on her hiney and slid down the snow covered ditch. Harper began with what always came to mind first and foremost – she began to pray. Lord, whatever or whoever was below, please let them be okay. She hoped she was in time.

CHAPTER 1

Dr. Crispin Steele was more than ready to escape the city and all the rushing to and fro for the holidays. He had been planning the trip back home for over three weeks. He had missed Thanksgiving because the hospital had been short staffed. His mom had given him three kinds of grief. Crispin knew if he did not make it home for the holidays, his mom would have his hide. Leaving the hospital, Crispin wished the staff Merry Christmas. He needed to get home, shower and pack. Crispin was a procrastinator. Everything was done at the last minute. Crispin worked better under stress. His goal was to get on the road no later than midnight. He needed this time. The holidays were his favorite but this road trip was more for his mom.

Crispin was ready for this trip. He not only missed his mom and dad, but he needed his mom and dad. He missed the hugs of his mom. He was a momma's boy and he was not afraid to admit it to his friends or his co-workers. Growing up, there had never been a time when Crispin had not seen his mom hugging friends and family. His mom had a way of making the day brighter with one of her hugs. Many times, Crispin did not want his mom to let him go. "The beauty of a hug" she told him "is more than the action." "It is knowing that the hug has encircled you into the warmth of feeling rescued. It is one heart lifting another because of the beautiful blend of kindness shared."

As he walked through his home checking the alarm system, his mind turned back to that one special day that Crispin had found true love. Crispin was not sure why that one Saturday morning, he turned around after passing the animal shelter BUT he did. When Crispin opened the door to the shelter of Endless Pawsabilities Rescue, there was no mistaking that everyone was excited. Crispin was immediately greeted by a young woman who was holding a kitten that looked to be the size of a teacup and then was holding the leash of what appeared to be a white bear attached to the other end. Crispin could not help but smile. The young lady smiled and told him to come in, have a seat and she would be right with him. Before Crispin could even respond, she turned and handed the small teacup kitten to the receptionist and the bulldog she was trying to convince to walk with her towards the back. The bulldog was not budging. And then he watched the tech pull a sprinkled donut from the box laying on the countertop. Immediately the beautiful bulldog sat. "Now Gertie", the tech began, "we had our walk, we've done our business and now it's time to go back in." Gertie, this was the bulldog's name. Crispin looked at the tech and then at Gertie. He took a step toward Gertie and knelt down. Without hesitation, Gertie placed her paw in Crispin's palm. He looked at the tech. "Is Gertie available for adoption?"

That memory brought Crispin back to the task at hand. Packing. Crispin had left a note for his housekeeper. He laid it on the table. He could feel the quiet. It had only been two weeks but it was different. She had left unexpectedly. Crispin did not know the cause that had taken her. Only that his days felt empty. As he had held her body in his arms that morning, Crispin knew that none could or would replace his one true love, Gertie. He sat down on the couch to reflect all that Gertie had given to him.

The routine had been to pull into his driveway, turn off the car, and immediately the barking would begin. Crispin could see the tip of her head through the front window. She was fighting the drapes. He would watch for the movement of the drapes. She would scoot the drapes to the side so she could get a better glimpse of Crispin. He could not wait to open the door. As he walked the path to the front porch, he knew she would be sitting in the middle of the foyer. This was his escape.

She was nothing like he had expected. She was the queen. Gertie ruled his household. Many a time, Crispin had made the decision that being a bachelor with a bulldog with no love interest had its advantages. Crispin had taken Gertie to the hospital on several occasions to meet the staff. The hospital staff would tease him that he only had eyes for Gertie. It was true. Crispin's career required a lot of attention. More than he could give a relationship. Even the worst day at the hospital, Crispin knew Gertie would make it all better. The love of an animal is unconditional. The love of a rescue is forever. Crispin had thought he was changing her life when in fact, Gertie had changed his. When he went to the shelter that one Saturday, Crispin had no idea what he would encounter. His Gertie had turned his world upside down and inside out.

There's an old saying that you can always sense when your child is in the room. You lay there realizing they are in the room but silently wishing that they will turn back around, head back to bed, and possibly sleep a few more minutes. Crispin knew if he made the tiniest of moves, there would be a scratch on the side of the bed with her paw. Gertie would not give up until Crispin rolled as close to the edge of the bed and peered down. Those big eyes were staring up at Crispin with a plea of "are you getting up now"? Crispin reached his hand towards Gertie, who immediately came up to nudge his hand and then place her paw in the air for Crispin to shake. This was how every morning began with Gertie.

Crispin had created a routine that fit both his and Gertie's lifestyles. Crispin would take Gertie for an early morning walk. There were approximately 52 steps from the front porch to Crispin's mailbox. That was it. That was as far as Gertie would travel. Along the way, she conducted her business and was ready to return inside. It brought a smile to Crispin's face whenever he would try to add something new to her routine. Gertie would stop dead in her tracks. She would not budge. The more Crispin would attempt to pull Gertie in the direction he needed her to walk, the more she would show him who the boss was. Crispin would encourage or tempt Gertie with a treat. The attempt did not go unnoticed by several of the neighbors. It had become a bet among the neighbors, as Crispin and Gertie were walking, if Gertie would move any additional steps or lead Crispin back home. The latter held true.

Crispin would hold the door wide and before he could even remove Gertie's harness leash, she was standing in front of the refrigerator door waiting for the treat that had been promised. Crispin had learned the hard way that if food and water were not served upon their return, Gertie would, by accident, turn the water dish and food dish upside down to draw attention to this fact. Crispin had stepped in the spilled water one too many times. A memory embedded deep into Crispin's favorite moments by Gertie due to the fact Crispin was wearing socks. Soggy socks were on Crispin's top three dislikes. The other two dislikes had also been created by Gertie.

It seemed that Gertie had a deep affection for donuts, especially the ones with sprinkles (this he had learned from the shelter the day he adopted Gertie). Crispin had discovered that when Gertie wanted something, there was no stopping her. Crispin discovered Gertie's intelligence when he had gone into the kitchen one night. The donuts from Sweet Sprinkles Bakery had been left on the kitchen table. They were a treat leftover from the workday. He had a craving for dessert after supper with a big ole glass of milk and Crispin knew these donuts would hit the spot. He had walked into the kitchen only to discover that as he was walking towards the box of donuts, something was sticking to his bare feet. Gertie was looking sideways at Crispin. He sat down on the kitchen floor to see what objects were glued to the bottom of his feet. As he glanced at one foot, Gertie had begun to inch closer to Crispin. Crispin began to smile. There was no mistaking what had taken place with Crispin's dessert. Gertie's lips were covered in what Crispin now knew were on his feet – SPRINKLES. Crispin gently reached for the baby wipes in the center of the table and cleaned Gertie. From that day forward, there was never a day that Gertie was without sprinkles.

He picked up his luggage beside the front door. Crispin did not look back.

CHAPTER 2

Harper had been around animals all of her life. Pictures in her parents' home could attest to that. There was the time her mom had received the telephone call from Harper's Kindergarten teacher inquiring if the family could baby sit the classroom mascot, Rufus, the guinea pig. Harper begged and pleaded and promised that she would be the one to take care of Rufus. Her mom laughed with affection. Of course, the family would love to baby sit Rufus during the Christmas break. Rufus, upon arrival, to the True home had taken the word "adventure" to a whole new level. There were times that Harper would take Rufus out of the cage and place him in the exercise ball, which was great except for the times, Rufus decided to roll down the steps. Poor thing. When the exercise ball came to a complete halt, Rufus seemed to have a bit of a dazed walk. His stance was just a bit off kilter. That little mishap took about five years off Harper's mom's life, in addition, to probably taking off of Rufus' life. Several times, they caught the cat, Sunny, taking Rufus for a roll, too. The worse was when they lost Rufus for several hours and for the life of them could not figure out where the exercise ball had rolled. It was only the evidence of Sunny walking behind the couch licking his paws as if he had just finished supper. Harper's mom pulled the couch from the wall, and there Rufus was. Sitting quietly in the ball, like a child being in placed in time out, waiting to roll away. Harper cherished these memories. Her pets had made her childhood full of adventure, love, and best of all, laughter.

Harper shook herself back to the task at hand. Rescue and transport. Harper was the chief veterinarian at the shelter known as Clip-n-Dales Rescue. Harper was very petite in size so when individuals of the male persuasion would see her wrangling a St. Bernard or a Bulldog, they were in utter amazement of the strength she possessed. Harper had learned if she wanted something done, and done the right way, she would just handle it. So much easier to circumvent all the criteria that went along with rescue. Being the only veterinarian in Yellow Springs, Colorado and, then of course, being the only female vet, Harper was the talk of the town. Harper did not mind. She relished the fact that she did not have to worry about competition in her hometown. Harper would go the extra mile for any animal. Her word and integrity is what she based the success of Clip-n-Dales Rescue.

The rescue that had put Harper on the map as the "best vet of all times" was when Harper received an in home rescue while having dinner with her mom and dad one evening after work. The door burst open and with hands flying in the air, Miss Yo and Mr. Jamie , stood in the doorway holding their favorite pet rooster, Cluck Norris. Both Miss Yo and Mr. Jamie were talking at the same time and the only words that Harper heard were "he lost his crow". Before Harper knew it, they had held Cluck out for her to examine.

Harper knew that she needed to do a full examination at her office but wanted to assess Cluck Norris before leaving. Her parents (Gilly and Zak) looked at Harper preparing to apologize. Harper winked at them. She knew what needed to be done. She took Cluck Norris from them. She began to rub the top of his head and motioned for Miss Yo and Mr. Jamie to follow her into the den. Everyone, including her mom and dad's chihuahuas (MeMe, Bruiser and Dillon), were in attendance to give an opinion. Harper smiled. All eyes were on her.

Seats were taken and eyes were glued to Harper as to the outcome of why Cluck Norris had lost his voice. Harper learned never to travel without her medical bag. But she also knew to keep a spare medical bag on hand at her parents. You never knew when an emergency would arrive. She held Cluck underneath her arm and reached for her bag on the floor to the side of the sofa. Harper had left strict instructions that the bag was not to be touched or removed. She reached in and pulled out her stethoscope in order to listen to Cluck's heart and throat. Harper heard a bit of gurgling but nothing too serious. She inquired as to what Cluck may have eaten throughout the day. Harper listened intently as the list went on and on. She smiled and then she handed Cluck back to Miss Yo and Mr. Jamie. She informed the family that she would need to run a scope to see if something was blocking Cluck's airway. Harper asked if 7 the next morning would work. Of course, they said. Needless to say after morning tests, and a bit of a warm water flush, Cluck Norris' crow returned. In Harper's experience, sometimes these things are just unexplainable and nature takes over, at least that's what she was diagnosing it as.

CHAPTER 3

Crispin did not mind the long drive. It afforded him more time to enjoy his favorite songs. The genre was that of the country music and Christmas and when you combined both of these, you couldn't go wrong. Crispin had taken the time before leaving to record about five hours worth of "driving" music. He had packed several Christmas gifts that he had purchased for his mom and dad. The rest he would take care of when he returned to Yellow Springs, Colorado.

Crispin loved the country side. When he had left home, there was just a hint in the air of the temps changing. Crispin thrived in the cold weather. The chill of the day was the best part of the holidays approaching. As soon as Crispin walked through the door at home, the scrubs came off and the sweats were pulled on. There was nothing better than sweat pants that were baggy and loose and a long sleeve tee to make the evening. Driving great distances was another opportunity to dress down. Looking at Crispin dressed so relaxed one would never know his profession. Crispin enjoyed surprising folk. Most thought him to be the playboy at the hospital. Only a few knew of his love for rescue and of those few, he could count on his hand his friends who knew that he was a "softie" when it came to Gertie.

There was a lot to think about on this particular drive home. So much had happened within six months. Changes at the hospital. Some Crispin agreed with and others, he would either have to accept or make a decision. Crispin loved pediatrics. He loved the staff at Lullaby Children's Hospital. They were one big family. Something Crispin had not experienced growing up. He was an only child. He also knew that when the time came, he would handle the care and provisions for both his parents. For the first time, Crispin had begun to realize that his mom and dad were aging. Time could not be turned back.

Crispin had been driving for several hours. It was in the early morning. The sky was just opening. He knew he was getting close to home because the roads were getting curvy. Plus, it had begun to snow. It was a heavy snow. Something he had not anticipated and something that the weatherman had missed. Crispin knew he was going to need to slow the car down. He needed to be aware of his surroundings. He hated to admit that he was a bit anxious to get home. It was this thought that would be his last thought. The car hit an ice patch on the road and began to fishtail. Crispin lost control and could only see the trees and ditch ahead.

Crispin could not open his eyes. His head was throbbing. He tried to shift his legs. Something was blocking his access. Why could he not move? The car was upside down. How long had he been in the ditch? He placed his hand on his head and realized that there was blood running down the side of his head. What did he hit? And then he heard the snow crunching. Something or someone was coming down the hill. Please, Lord, Crispin began to pray, let it be a person. The crunching grew closer and then he heard the voice. He saw the legs coming into sight. Then the body bent down. He could hear a voice. It was a woman's voice. She was asking him "Are you okay. Can you let me know where you're hurt? Are you okay?" Crispin could only mutter the words in a labored voice "Help me."

CHAPTER 4

Harper could tell that the situation was dangerous. The call to 911 had been placed. As she slid down the hill, she noticed the vehicle was upside down. She had no idea how many were inside the flipped car. The fur babies were whining. Harper knew they sensed what she knew. Time was of the essence. As she approached the vehicle, she could hear a soft moan. She knelt down and a hand reached for hers. She fell back into the snow from being caught off guard. It was a man. He was alive. The only way Harper could assess the situation was to lay down on her stomach in the snow to speak with the injured individual. She lay down and Harper then noticed that he had never let go of her hand. She placed her hand on top of his.

"Can you tell me your name?" "Do you remember what happened?" Harper placed her hand on his to see if there was any blood. As she pulled her hand back, she knew the answer. Harper could feel that her hand was moist. Now to find out where the blood was coming from. Before Harper could return her hand, the man began to speak. "I'm Dr. Crispin Steele. I lost control of my car. I think the blood is coming from the side of my head. I hit the steering wheel pretty hard. The air bag parachuted open. I feel this is where the blood has originated."

Dr. Steele may have had a wreck, but he was very thorough in his own self-examination. Harper asked if he were hurt anywhere else. Was he able to move his arms and legs. Crispin informed Harper "I don't think anything is broken." Harper knew better than to move him. She turned to find all three of the fur babies looking down at her with heads tilted as if to say "Well, is he okay or not?" They had not left.

Off in the distance, Harper heard the sirens of rescue. It always seemed in rescue that it took forever for help to arrive. When in real time, it was probably less than ten minutes. As the noise of the sirens became louder, Harper was prayerful they would see her vehicle. She peered into the window to check on Dr. Crispin Steele. "Dr. Steele, EMS and the Fire Department have arrived. Rescue is on its way."

Crispin heard the female voice. Hearing the female voice holler as to her location, Crispin knew that she was making them aware of their location. Crispin realized he could only lay there. He did not know what was restricting his movement but he knew he was trapped. He could not move. Crispin heard the crunch of shoes. He knew she was going to guide the EMS and FD to where he was located. He did not know why, but he did not want "HER" to leave. He did not know if anxiety had taken over or if shock were setting in. He reached for her. His hand reaching for hers. He just needed to touch and be reassured she would not leave him. His last words before he lost consciousness were "Please rescue me."

CHAPTER 5

Harper knew the EMS and fire department were close. The noise of the sirens blaring were getting louder as they approached. At the top of the hill, her vehicle was still resting. At the bottom of the hill, his vehicle was upside down. She needed to leave for just a few minutes in order to grab their attention so they would not pass them up. As she started to gather the wawas and make the track back up the hill, she reached for his hand. "I promise I'll be right back." She did not know why, but anxiety began to build. He had lost consciousness. She grabbed the three little hoodlums that had been patiently waiting for Harper to make the first move. She motioned for them to come to her and without any hesitation, all three were standing at her feet. It was a good thing that Harper had worn a big snow jacket. She never knew when she would have to stuff a few rescues inside for warmth and containment. Thank you, Lord, for the intuition given. As Harper picked up the wawas and zipped them safely inside, a noise caught her attention.

Harper knew the vehicles had stopped. She could no longer hear their engines. At the top of the hill was her best friend and Chief of the EMS, Ginny Lynn. Harper waved and motioned her to come down. Ginny acknowledged. Before she began the descent down the hill, Ginny turned to Red. She gave him orders of what to bring down the hill with him and the crew.

Harper waited until Ginny had reached the bottom. Ginny looked at her best friend. Wherever Harper was, there was a story. Most of the stories began with "I had to rescue them" and the adventure began from there. Harper told Ginny as quick as she could what had transpired in the last thirty minutes. They both raced to the upside down vehicle. The rest of the staff were coming down the incline with equipment in hand, along with the back board because of possible head injuries as Harper had relayed over the 911 call.

Harper stepped back. She knew better than to stand in Ginny's way. Ginny was not just efficient but was thorough in her investigation. Ginny motioned for Red to bring the back board and told him to bring the jaws of life, too. They needed to cut the doctor out from the vehicle. Ginny looked at Harper "How do you know he's a doctor?" "Do we know his name?" "His name is Dr. Crispin Steele, that's all I got."

Ginny bent down and began to ask Dr. Steele the typical questions: "Can you hear me? Do you know where you are? Do you know what happened?' There was a bit of mumbling but Ginny did not like the fact that Dr. Steele could not respond coherently to her questions.

Ginny turned to look for Red. He was right there with equipment and board. "I got it, Miss Ginny. You just need to step out of the way." Red went to work. It was that quick. It was that fast. Dr. Crispin Steele was on the backboard. Ginny whistled to inform the crew at the top, they need the rope. It was too dangerous to lift and carry Dr. Steele up the hill.

Red began tightening the straps and then ran the rope through all appropriate loops to keep Dr. Steele in position. He looked up and threw the thumbs up in the air for the crew to begin the pull of the backboard.

Ginny motioned for Harper. "Come on, it's time to go. Do we need to grab anything from inside his vehicle or are we good?" Harper briefly peered inside the window that had busted. She did not know if she needed to gather anything. Better to leave as is and not disturb anything. More than likely the wrecker service in town would be called but right now, the wawas were getting antsy and she wanted to be sure Dr. Crispin Steele was going to be okay.

CHAPTER 6

Crispin could feel tugging on his body. He could tell that this was not a female. The voice that told Crispin just to lay still. This was a man. This was not the same voice that he had begged not to leave him. The voice informed Crispin that rescue would take care of everything from this point. Crispin heard the car door squeaking. It was being manipulated to get it to open. He heard a female voice, but again, not the original one. "Rip it. We need to get him free so we can examine any injuries. Crispin knew he was injured.

The board had been slid under his body so there was easier access to get Crispin assessed. Crispin heard two female voices. There she was. She was in the conversation. He could tell by the tone of her voice when describing what she had discovered. Hearing her voice placed a sense of security over Crispin. She would take care of him. She had promised not to leave him. He could not open his eyes.

Everyone was secured and seated in the ambulance. Vitals had been checked. Ginny gave Harper the thumbs up and then the nod, which Harper knew was the send off. Ginny had told Harper they would take him immediately to Grand Oak General Hospital. Harper nodded and waved. Harper knew she needed to get the wawas back to the shelter. She would check on the good Dr. Steele at the end of her day. She would pray that all was well. She picked up the wawas and placed them in the back seat. This is where the day had started but where would it end?

The ambulance pulled into the entrance of the ER at Grand Oak General Hospital. Ginny and crew were met with the typical questions. How serious? Could the individual speak? Was there anyone with him? What was his name? Crispin heard everything but yet he felt so tired. He could barely keep his eyes open. I need to tell them who I am he thought to himself. His mom and dad were expecting him. If he were late, he knew his mother would flip like a light switch. On and off would not come close to describing his mom's emotions and worry.

Crispin had learned growing up that his mom always had a sixth sense with matters that related specifically to Crispin, especially, when it came to girlfriends. Crispin did not know how she did it, but his mom always knew when things were not right in his love life. Crispin knew she had hoped he would find the "one" who would turn his life inside out. Crispin also realized that his mom and dad were not getting any younger, and, of course, he was not either but inevitably, grandchildren were always brought up when a visit was made. His mom never showed disappointment in the fact that Crispin was still a bachelor. She always told him love was just around the corner. He just had not turned the corner yet.

Ginny had left all the info on Dr. Crispin Steele at the ER registration desk, at least what she could gather from Dr. Steele, who was not much help, since he was in and out of consciousness. From what Ginny could surmise, he was a pediatric doctor coming home to visit his parents. She had looked at his hand. Nope, no ring. Of course, that didn't mean anything. She had looked to see if there was the slightest bit of indentation around that "ring" finger. Nope, no indentation. Lord, if he woke up while she had been surveying him, she did not know if she could come up with a legitimate excuse. From what the observations and vitals had been on the drive to the hospital, he was not in any danger. A few broken bones and bruising from the impact, but overall, he should be ok. Time to leave and hit headquarters to check in, Ginny told the crew.

CHAPTER 7

As Harper pulled up to the rescue, she knew she was running late. Dan was outside walking one of the dogs. She could tell that Dan was having a bit of difficulty convincing Mugsy, (a German Shepherd) to do his business so they could return inside. Mugsy was enjoying himself. Dan was not. Harper put her vehicle into park. Made sure the wawas were ready. Opened the back driver's side door and watched as they waited for Harper to pick them up and place them in their stroller-carrier. Spoiled little nuggets. "Fine, okay, I'll pick you up, but only this time," she told all three. She knew that was a lie. She pulled the stroller from the floor board and popped it open. One by one she placed them inside. Dan was holding the entry door, with Mugsy sitting patiently by his side, for Harper and the fur babies.

Dan commented smiling, "Can't wait to hear the story this morning. This should be a doozie." Harper stated with a calm voice, "The wawas had to tinkle, pulled over, let them out, heard something, car upside down, found a good looking man, he's a doctor, Ginny got him out, he should be at the hospital by now."

Dan chuckled, "Well that was more than a doozie, that was one of those mic drops." "Trust me", Harper stated, "The mic dropped and the batteries fell out."

Mercedes, the medical assistant, greeted everyone with a smile. "Well…well…look what the cat drug in." Both Harper and Dan looked at each other and just smiled. "Come on guys, you know that saying never gets old, especially since we work in rescue. Oh, lawd, just give me this one. It's early morning and I can tell that Dr. True has already had one heck of a morning." Dan turned and looked at Mercedes, "Fine, it's funny, you win. Let's get this day started. I can hear Mugsy's belly growling which means only ONE thing. He's famished as always." Mercedes grinned and saluted Dan. "On this day like a tailored suit." Dan began walking Mugsy down the hallway and hollered to Harper, "Doc, we really gotta work on her delivery with these quirky sayings. Don't forget, I'll need additional details about the good looking doctor," Dan stated.

Harper had begun placing the wawas on the floor from the stroller. She looked at Mercedes and winked. Mercedes' eyebrows drew up. "A doctor and you said a good looking doctor". Harper laughed. "Later, we will discuss much later." "Who's up to bat first?" Harper asked. Mercedes knew when Dr. True was skirting the issue. This was one of those times. Mercedes loved her job and she loved rescue even more. Yes, the day had begun. Details to follow.

CHAPTER 8

"Dr. Steele, are you ready? Just one more day and your family can bust you out of here. I promise," Addilynn stated. Crispin was in the bathroom, brushing his teeth to begin the day's events. He was the patient. He had to keep reminding himself of this. "Promises, promises, that's all I've heard since I've been here. And yet, I'm still here. What's wrong with this picture?" Crispin teased her. Addilynn chuckled. He had been a handful when he arrived. After going through all the x-rays, the CT scans, the MRIs, Dr. Crispin Steele's injuries were only a broken leg, in addition to minor scratches and bruising from the soft tissue injuries sustained while the car flipped. Crispin's stay at Grand Oak General Hospital was top notch. From the staff to the doctors, all had been attentive and thorough with his medical needs; specifically, with his recuperation and therapy.

Crispin's family had been contacted. Before a room could be assigned for Crispin, his mom was bursting through the door of the ER, not screaming, but demanding where her son was. Behind his mom, was Crispin's dad, smiling and just nodding his head and saying hello and how pleasant it was to see everyone. It was nice to live in a small town where everyone knew everybody and everything that took place (sometimes). Crispin's dad knew better than to interfere with Crispin's mom when her anxiety was on high alert. Especially, when it related to their one and only son, Dr. Crispin Steele.

Mr. and Mrs. Steele had met with the doctors that had been assigned to Crispin and his medical recovery. By the end of the meeting, a plan had been set in motion by Crispin's mom. All that was needed was the approval of the doctors. Crispin knew better than to argue with his mom when she was focused. There was no changing her mind.

Crispin had grown up to appreciate his mom's no non-sense way of thinking. She was able to get more done in an hour than most folk in an entire work day of 8 hours. Crispin knew that his mom had been counting the days until Crispin would be coming home. She would remind Crispin of the fact that his room was waiting and she would be the one taking care of him.

After a few encounters with his mom, the staff, nurses and even the doctors knew just to nod their head and agree. Crispin's dad did not miss a beat either. Crispin's dad supported his mom in all that she wanted to do (within reason, of course he would tell Crispin) but most of her ideas and ventures, his dad was gung ho. This is what Crispin loved about his parents. They truly supported each other and their dreams.

Crispin was brought back to the task at hand. Therapy. Addilynn picked up her clipboard and inquired as to who was leading the way. Like Crispin did not know that they watched his gait to make sure that his leg was mending. Addilynn tilted her head. "Really, after this last day, you're still gonna ask, Dr. Steele. You know I have to watch your balance as you navigate the walk towards therapy. So I'm not looking at your butt, I'm watching your leg and its movement. So by all means, lead the way, Dr. Steele." Crispin raised his brow in shock and laughed. "Well, I have a great looking butt, too, just in case you needed to be reminded."

If felt like a month that Crispin had been in the hospital and in therapy when in actuality it had only been four days. It was time to leave. Crispin knew he would need to call his mom to come pick him up when he was released. His car had been totaled which presented another item to take care of on the "to do list" when returning to his parents' home. He needed a vehicle.

Crispin finished therapy and Addilynn gave him a thumbs up. She walked him back to his room. Addilynn wished him well and a Merry Christmas. Crispin looked at Addilynn and asked her the only question he did not have answer. "Addilynn" he began, "who rescued me?" Addilynn looked at him and said "Dr. Steele, I'm sorry, I have no idea, but I bet you're grateful to whoever it was." Crispin nodded he understood. All he knew was his rescuer was a female and had pets.

CHAPTER 9

Harper was not just whooped. She was boogered out. Numerous times this week, she had driven back to the shelter in the middle of the night to check on the new arrivals. Rescue was difficult on everyone. Getting acclimated to new surroundings and new voices. The week had been more of "taking in" than "letting go". The shelter was almost to maximum capacity which Harper knew was not good. She was going to have to come up with a big Adopt-a-Thon fundraiser weekend. Every one of the fur babies that were in the shelter's care needed a home. Several had just been brought in and still needed to be vetted. And others had been there for several weeks to a few months. There was one though, that for some unknown reason, kept getting passed by. Harper figured it could have been due to the fact she was not a puppy, but was considered more a "senior". There had been several inquiries on the Chihuahua but no takers as of yet. Harper knew her time was coming. There was someone out there for this fur baby. Someone that would give her all the love and attention that she deserved.

The front entry door opened and Harper heard Mercedes holler "It's just me, the hunk has left the building. Are you ready to close up shop? Harper stopped in her tracks. "The what had left the what?" she inquired of Mercedes. "Oh you know, HIM. Everyone is talking about him. Dr. Crispin Steele. Word on the corner is he has been released and will be heading to his parents' home."

Harper felt her stomach jump. Not as in upset but more as in excitement. He had been released. She had not asked any questions about his progress at the hospital. Harper didn't need to. The entire town was talking about "that sexy doctor". Harper knew who they were referring to. Geeze, it wasn't like he was the ONLY male in the town of Yellow Springs.

Mercedes watched the emotions on Harper face when she stated he was out and referred to him as "the hunk." She did not want to ask Harper if she was even curious how the good doctor was faring. She knew Harper wanted to know. Mercedes had kept tabs on the town gossip of "that sexy doctor." She would drop a few hints here and there just to see Harper play the disinterested by passer. Mercedes knew different. Something had taken place between Harper and "the hunk."

"Everything looks good, Mercedes. Thank you for your help today. Let's take one more quick peek and lock it up for the night."

As they walked out together, Harper turned and locked the door and began walking with Mercedes to their vehicles. "You know, he's headed back to his parents to stay for the holidays. Or at least that's what I've heard tell. Might be a good time to stop by and introduce yourself. You did rescue him," Mercedes stated matter of fact.

Harper grinned. She knew what Mercedes was up to. Harper did, in fact, think about checking in on him at his parents' home. Harper knew his parents from the charitable fundraisers that had been held in town. They had been in attendance at several of the shelter's events. They had been generous with their donation and Harper truly appreciated that. Stopping by and introducing herself was a big step. Right now, her identity had remained anonymous. For the moment, she wanted to keep it that way. Harper did not know why, but she was not ready to reveal herself to Dr. Crispin Steele.

CHAPTER 10

Crispin knew as soon as they pulled into the driveway, his mom would insist on him taking a nap. Crispin smiled. He was not a little boy anymore who needed naps but when he thought about it, he was just a tad bit tired. May be a quick cat nap. Crispin opened the passenger car door. As he stood up and stepped out of the car, he looked around at his parent's home. This was his home. This is where love was found. This was what he needed.

Working in the city, there were no piles of leaves waiting to be jumped in during the fall. There were not any mornings where the dew was still glistening off the grass. The smell of fresh cut grass during summer was like being in a chocolate chip cookie store – just the aroma brought back memories of his childhood.

Crispin looked over at his mom. She was getting teary eyed. She had been watching him. As his mom was aging, Crispin had noticed she was become more sentimental and emotional about small things. He winked at her. "Mom, I love you, you know that. Forever and a day."

His mom nodded. "Of course, you do. You're my only child, it's required." Crispin chuckled. "Come on, let's go inside where Dad is waiting. I know you think I need to rest, so for today, I'll give into you."

They walked up the sidewalk. Crispin's dad had heard the car pull into the driveway. He was standing in the doorway. "Well, come on in. I've got a snack. Your mom has already prepared your room from top to bottom."

Walking inside, Crispin felt as if he had stepped back in time. The memories of coming home from high school and being greeted by the family pet, Alex (Crispin's chow chow) flooded his mind. Alex had been a huge part of Crispin's middle and high school years. This was heaven.

Crispin could smell the chili. His dad was famous for his chili in the community (especially at the big chili cook off benefiting a different charity each year). His dad had placed runner up several times but the grand prize had eluded him. Best part about his Dad's chili, there was spaghetti in there. What better way to eat chili than with spaghetti and off to the side on a plate were the crackers and peanut butter sandwiches. Crispin thought to himself, I'm never leaving.

His mom motioned him to go ahead and sit down. When his dad had placed the meal on the table and sat down, his mother tapped for Crispin's hand to hold. Prayer. Thanks for what the Lord had given and blessed them with. This was the one prayer that Crispin's mom insisted on. There was no way around it. Crispin's mom once told him, "It doesn't take that long to say two simple words 'thank you', does it?" Crispin could not argue with that or with his Mom.

Crispin pushed his chair back. The rule at home was whoever cooked was exempt from cleaning. Whoever ate the meal, needed to help clear away. Even though the year was 2020, Crispin's mom did not have a dishwasher. Her thinking was why have a dishwasher when she could do this household chore herself. Plus that dishwasher set the electric bill just a few dollars higher. No need to spend when you didn't have to. Crispin's mom was sensible to a fault. His dad used to mouth the words "just nod your head in agreement." Crispin had done a lot of "nodding".

As dusk was approaching, Crispin and his parents walked out to the deck and sat down to watch the sun fade. Crispin's mom reached for his hand. "I'm glad you're home, honey. Tomorrow is a new day, get some rest. Tomorrow your dad and I want to take you into town for a surprise." Crispin stood up and kissed his Mom on her cheek. He was a momma's boy. He loved his Mom more than life itself.

CHAPTER 11

The morning sun was peeking into Harper's window. Why was it so bright? What time was it? This was Saturday, correct? She was going in late to the shelter. She was about to pull the cover over her head to darken the room when the phone rang. There was only ONE person who would call so early in the morning and that could only be the shelter. There were only a handful of folk that had Harper's cell. Mercedes being one of them. Harper answered "Good morning, Mercedes. Pray tell, what's happening this morning?" Mercedes laughed. "Just reminding you we have several rescues coming in this morning and it's Furry Scurry Saturday Adoption Day, or did you forget?"

No, I did not forget, how could I? You've been planning all week. Your enthusiasm is contagious. I'm on my way. Let me throw my hair up in a bun and I'll be there in 20 minutes," Harper told Mercedes. "Make it 10, we already have a line," Mercedes squealed and hung the phone up.

Harper could not believe that folk were already in line for the big adoption day. Harper loved her town. All were willing to help wherever needed. Any type of charity event or fundraiser, the town folk came out in droves.

Harper brushed her tooth, washed her face, threw some deodorant on, pulled her hair on top of her head, sweats on – she was ready. Grabbed a bottled water and the box of donuts off the kitchen counter top. Jumped in the shelter's SUV and was off to the shelter.

Crispin smelled breakfast. His mom was cooking his favorite meal of the day. Boy, he sure hoped it was everything that he loved. He could not remember the last time he had a home-cooked meal. Working in one of the top hospitals for pediatrics, he never had time to sit down and enjoy his food. Time was limited. He showered and then returned to the kitchen where his Mom was setting the table and his Dad was watching the early morning news. "It's ready, let's eat, come on sweetheart. Crispin has showered. It's going to get cold if we don't sit, pray and eat, NOW," Crispin's mom put the emphasis on NOW.

It was the best breakfast. Pancakes, sausage, biscuits, gravy, buttered syrup, and orange juice. Crispin was never returning to Lullaby Children's Hospital.

He watched as his mom and dad both cleared away the table. Left the dishes in the sink and said "Are you ready for your surprise?" Crispin truly did not know what they had up their sleeve but he was game. "Absolutely!"

Out the door they went. Loaded up in his parents' car and began the drive to….Crispin did not know where they were going. "Mom, we are going where?" "You just have to wait. I know you're going to love it," Crispin's mom stated with a cheekish grin.

Crispin knew his mom was trying to keep a secret about the morning. Why though, he was not for sure. His dad had not even shared what may be happening this morning. Christmas music was playing as they drove into town. It was a cold overcast morning with the anticipation of snow (not any accumulation) but possible flurries according to the local weatherman.

As Crispin's mom parked the car, Crispin noticed the town was beginning to look a lot like Christmas. It was then that he noticed that they had parked in front of a pet store. Nope, it was not a pet store but a shelter of sorts or it could be a doctor's office. Crispin looked at his mom. She was beaming from ear to ear. "This is it. Come on." Crispin's view went to the name of the business: "Clip-n-Dales Rescue". Before Crispin could say anything, his Mom had opened the door and disappeared inside. When he and his Dad walked in, everyone was greeted with a "hello Mr. and Mrs. Steele, welcome back. Have you come to check out the new intakes or did you want to see if you know who was still here?" Crispin could not help but smile. The young lady behind the counter was motioning for them to come down the hallway. Barking. Loud barking. That's all that Crispin heard. And it was not just loud, but it was a deep husky bark. "Good morning, my name is Mercedes. I am the Vet Tech and Receptionist. And you are?" Crispin thought to himself, isn't she just the syrup on the ice cream. He could not help but look at Mercedes from head to toe. "And good morning to you, too. I'm Dr. Crispin Steele and evidently you know my parents," Crispin informed her. "I do. They volunteer once at week at the shelter. We can tell they love the rescues. Your mom and dad don't mind getting their fingernails dirty."

As Crispin was continuing the conversation with Mercedes, he heard another female voice speaking to his parents. "Couldn't stay away could you, Mr. and Mrs. Steele. I'm so happy to see you've returned. Did you come back to check on him? Or had someone else captured your attention?"

Crispin stopped dead in his tracks. That voice. He knew that voice. He had heard that voice before. Where? Was he imagining this? He shook his head and walked immediately to where the conversation was flowing. His mom and dad were deep in discussion with "that" voice. He could not see for her back was turned.

He heard her say "All three have been with me since I returned from Little Sandy Rescue. Remember, Mercedes, that's the day I ran into the flipped vehicle."

Crispin was frozen. What were the chances this was the ONE who rescued him. He walked towards his parents and then stood between them. Crispin cleared his throat. "So you're the ONE?"

Harper could not move. She couldn't even turn to face him. What were the odds that he would ever find Harper. What were the odds he would walk into her rescue? Better yet, what was she going to do?

"I am. I am Dr. Harper True. This is my rescue and office. I wondered after Ginny, the EMS director and staff dropped you off, what had happened. Well, I do not need to wonder any longer now, do I? Here you stand before me," Harper stated.

As Harper was stating the facts of the matter, Crispin could not help but admire Dr. Harper True. She was petite in frame with blonde curly hair and big green eyes. Never before have eyes held such danger and beauty all at once. She was exquisite. Dr. Harper True had a titillating pout to her lips that would draw any man's attention. Crispin wondered what it would be like to nibble her lips and make them swell with desire.

Harper stopped. She knew Dr. Crispin Steele was surveying her. More than likely, he was trying to piece together that morning and the role that Harper played. Harper began with, "Do you remember anything about that accident?"

"I know I lost control in the snow and flipped over the side of the road and landed upside down at the bottom. I remember a woman with the voice of an angel remained with me the entire time. After that, it gets a little bit fuzzy."

"Yes, Dr. Steele, that was our Harper," Mercedes began. "We wondered why she was so late arriving at the office that day and now we know." Mercedes winked at Dan as he turned the corner to see what all the commotion was about.

Dan greeted Crispin's parents with familiarity and then extended his hand to Crispin. As he was shaking Crispin's hand, he turned and said "So, this is the "sexy doctor" everyone has been talking about?"

Crispin watched as Harper's expression was one of dismay and quite comical as she smacked her forehead. Harper started to say something to Mercedes, but instead, Crispin caught her off guard with the comeback "So you think I'm sexy, Dr. True?"

Okay, things were not only getting out of hand, Harper was actually blushing and he knew it. Before Harper could make a profound statement, she watched as Crispin's mom smiled and pointed her finger at Crispin "behave", she told him. "Dr. True, we are here to see who needs a bit of playtime and a possible morning stroll."

Okay. Dodged that with ease, Harper thought to herself. "We just had a few to come in yesterday, as a matter of fact. Come on, I'll give Dr. Steele the tour of the rescue, as we walk and talk." Harper reached to open the door to lead the way when Dr. Steele reached for the handle as well.

As their hands touched, Harper felt the heat course through her veins. Was the air-conditioning turned on? She jerked her hand back and began to massage it. What was happening to her? Blushing and now perspiring. Was she coming down with something? Did she have a fever?

Crispin knew why she jerked her hand from his touch. He had felt it. It was like a bolt of lightning. He felt the electricity between he and Harper. Better to play it safe and act as if nothing had happened.

Harper began the introductions to each rescue as they approached. Crispin immediately noticed that his mom and dad had each chosen a "special" rescue to discuss how their day was going. He watched as Harper knelt down to greet each one and pet them for an acknowledgement.

As he came to the end, he noticed there was a big white ball of fur in a corner of the cage. Harper walked up behind him. "I will not separate them. They are bonded and all three must go together." Crispin did a double-take. "Three, I only see one, what are you talking about?" And then, Harper stooped down and reached her hand in and motioned in a wave and called "Bebe, Lily, Mikee, come here and introduce yourselves. I want you to meet the man we rescued." And then it made sense to Crispin. He knew there was someone else that day with Dr. True, but could not remember. It was these three little chihuhuas. Crispin knew the answer before he asked, and he was sure she had been asked many times, but he had to. "Why will you not separate them?"

Harper opened the pin and all three came running towards her. "Because Bebe is the mom and the other two are her pups (Lily and Mikee). They were found on the side of a road inside a taped box. Like, I said, don't even ask, they all go together." Crispin waved in his hands in the air. "No, no, you're good and I understand. I just wanted to know their story. We all have a story, Dr. True, of how we were rescued and by who."

Harper turned to look Crispin. She did not know why, but she was at ease sharing the wawas' story. There were not many folk that would listen to her stories of rescue. He seemed genuinely interested. That made an impression on Harper. Plus, as she was watching him, the wawas had taken up residence in his lap on the shelter floor.

Harper looked at Bebe, Lily and Mikee and told them that if Dr. Steele got out of hand to let her know. She had to check on a few others but would return. Dan had walked in and had begun his morning chores of cleaning, feeding and inventorying supplies. This was a daily task. It could not be shoved under the carpet, so to speak, but the animals deserved all that Harper and the rescue could afford to keep them safe, warm, and most of all – loved.

As Dan was cleaning, Crispin placed the wawas back in their pin. He walked towards Dan and said "What do you need help with?" Dan smiled. It was folk like this that kept the shelter afloat. There was not enough dollars to hire extra help so Harper depended on the community to give when they could and how they could.

"First, we need to gather all the pee pads in each pen that has been soiled. Sweep and then hot mop the floors. We then need to get clean water for their bowls. I'll get the food for each rescue. We need to change out the linens on their beds. We can let those whose pens we are cleaning to run outside." Dan held out the broom for Crispin to retrieve. Without hesitation, Crispin bent down to pick up the pads, pitched them in the trash cart, and began mopping.

Crispin's mom and dad observed what had just taken place. They had raised a compassionate son and one that loved animals. Crispin looked up as they approached him. "We are gonna get a quick bite to eat, would you like something. We'll check with Dan, Mercedes and Dr. True on the way out and get them lunch, too. "Just grab me a sandwich, chips and drink, please, Mom." Dan placed his order. Crispin could hear his parents talking to Mercedes and then Harper to get their orders. They would not be back for about an hour, which gave Crispin time to get to know a bit more information about Dr. Harper True and who she truly was.

CHAPTER 12

Harper had given her lunch order to Crispin's parents. Such nice folk. They were always thinking of others first. They were the first ones to volunteer to help if the shelter needed anything. Harper had grown up with the bible verse of Acts 20:35. They sure exemplified what these words meant. Harper turned to walk through the doors to the kennel where she knew Dan and Crispin were cleaning. It was not just one that made a difference. Harper had been blessed with good employees who understood what the word rescue entailed – one of the biggest being time.

She placed her had on the door to push through. Harper had no idea that Crispin was pushing through on the other side. Even more so was the fact that Crispin had an arm load of pee pads that he needed to discard. At the same time, Crispin butted into Harper and both fell to the ground. Pee pads flew in the air. Crispin turned to catch Harper. Harper fell into Crispin's chest and both landed on the floor. It could not have been orchestrated any better, Crispin thought to himself, as he looked up into those big green eyes. Harper looked down at Crispin. Her hands were on his chest to keep her balance. Her hands were on his rock hard chest. Before Harper could think of anything else, Crispin gave her a light kiss unable to resist. When she did not pull away, Crispin placed his hand on the back of Harper's neck and pulled her closer. The kiss was unexpected. The kiss was soft as if he were testing her. Harper did not know what had overcome her. But she did not want the kiss to stop. The kiss began softly but was quickly gaining passion. Harper returned his kiss with a fevered excitement of the unknown. Crispin needed to taste the delicate woman that was laying on top of him. Harper felt herself breathless. The intensity of the kiss and the firmness of his touch, Harper knew she was messing with fire but it felt good and so right. Just when Harper thought she was drowning, both she and Crispin heard the feet and then the voice.

"Do I need to call rescue?" Dan inquired, holding back his smile. Harper rolled off Crispin and jumped up and told him "No, Crispin was entering the kennel and I was exiting. We bumped into each other coming through at the same time.

"Okay, so that's what we're calling it now. Bumping. That works for me." Dan raised his eyebrows in surprise and then winked at both. Crispin was still lying on the floor grinning up at Harper. "Was it good for you because it sure was good for me?" Harper did not want to smile but this bantering going back and forth with the sexual innuendo was too much. She threw her hands in the air. "Not even going to touch that with a ten foot pole."

As Crispin was standing, Mercedes hollered from the front office "lunch has arrived". Crispin's parents had walked in just at the right moment. Brown paper bags in hand along with drink carrier. Harper had to admit she was hungry. Plus she needed the down time to gather herself after falling on top of Crispin. Harper was feeling just a bit flustered. Lunch was spread on the table in the breakroom. Crispin's mom was busy finding plates, napkins, utensils and setting the table. The shelter breakroom had never smelt so good. Mismatched chairs were pulled to the table. Crispin's mom looked around and said, everything is ready.

"Let's say grace and chow down. We don't want the food to get cold."

Crispin leaned across the table to grab the ketchup. Harper reached for the ketchup at the same time. Crispin looked at her and said "Let go, I had dibs first." "No, you didn't. You weren't even close to reaching," Harper pouted. Crispin took his thumb and began to caress Harper's thumb on the bottle. "Pout much more like that and you can have anything you desire," Crispin whispered so only Harper could hear. Harper did not know why, but she could not remove her hand. Shoot, she didn't think she could move. She was stuck to the chair and her hand was glued to the ketchup bottle. Harper was hot. Geeze, what was going on, Harper thought to herself. Crispin watched Harper's reaction to his words. Her cheeks had become flush. Her eyes were as bright as a precious gem. And, she was still touching Crispin's hand and holding on to that bottle of ketchup. Crispin could tell she was uncomfortable with the situation, especially after that last remark.

"You can let go. I'll share with you," Crispin grinned. Before Harper could wipe that grin off his face, she heard the front door open and the frantic voice of male. "Help, please help me." Immediately, Harper jumped into action with Mercedes right behind. When they entered the lobby, they were met with the desperate pleas of Aaron with his basset hound, Fred. Aaron was holding Fred in his arms. Harper could tell he was trying not to panick. She told Mercedes to get the ER prepared. She looked at Aaron. "Tell me what happened." Aaron took a deep breath. "I only left the room for a minute. I had left the kitchen sink cabinet open where our cleaning supplies were stored. He must have been snooping around. I heard a thud and then I raced back to the kitchen. The cleaning solution had spilled on the floor. From what I can gather, Fred had licked part of the spill. He began to foam at the mouth and began to seize. I grabbed him and drove as fast as I could." The entire time that Aaron had been describing the details, Harper was examining Fred. Any time poison took place, time was of the essence to remove all the poison that had been ingested. They were going to need to pump Fred's stomach. Harper looked at Aaron. She informed him in a calm voice as to what the next step was going to be. She asked Aaron if he understood. Mercedes had taken Fred back while Harper prepared the treatment needed to save him.

Crispin remained to the side of the room. He watched Harper and how she handled the crisis. He also was impressed with her compassion and calmness to assess the situation so Aaron would not become more distraught about Fred.

As she turned to go to the ER, she told Aaron to go ahead and take a seat. She would return with an update. Harper then motioned to Crispin. "I need you."

CHAPTER 13

Crispin followed Harper's lead. She threw the scrubs at him and told him "You're scrubbing in, I need you." Crispin went into action. Within less than five seconds, he had placed the scrubs over his casual clothing and was ready to assist. Harper looked at Crispin. "Let's go."

Harper opened the door to the ER. Mercedes had Fred on the operating table. She had the medicine ready to be administered that would make Fred begin the process of throwing up. The goal was to get him to emit all the toxins that he had ingested. When Crispin walked towards Fred, he lifted his paw for Crispin to touch. Crispin began to rub Fred's paw. Fred eyes looked at Crispin. He had seen that look before. It was fear of the unknown. Fred's breathing became rapid. Harper knew she needed to get Fred to swallow the medicine and then wait for the meds to take effect. She looked at Crispin and pointed "The peanut butter is over there. Can you put some on a plastic spoon and then dip the pill so it's covered." Crispin did as instructed. He looked at Fred. "I'm right here with you. I'm not going anywhere." Crispin handed the spoon to Harper. Harper began to pet Fred. "Buddy, I just need you to be a good boy and take your medicine." She held the spoon upside down so that Fred would lick it. Crispin watched as Harper coaxed Fred. Her voice was gentle and soothing. One slurp and the pill was swallowed. Now the waiting game would begin. Harper informed Crispin that this would take approximately 15-20 minutes. The sooner, the better.

Harper told Mercedes that she would be fine and to head on home. Mercedes looked at Crispin whispering to Fred and then at Harper. "Are you sure?" Harper winked. "I'm sure. I'll walk out with you and inform Aaron we are staying the night and that we will call with any updates." As Mercedes was walking to the waiting area, where Aaron had been placed, she stopped abruptly. "We....what do you mean we.....who's we?"

Harper did not realize that she had said "we". "I'm good, Mercedes. I'll be fine. Did that sound better?" Mercedes knew that Harper was not going to budge. "No. I'll tell Aaron he can head on home and YOU will call if there is any change." As Mercedes was informing Aaron of the up to date status, Harper walked to the door to let them both out. "Kicking us out or asking us to leave?", Mercedes grinned. "I'm kicking you both out. If anything occurs, I'll call you Aaron. Fred is in good hands." Harper locked the entrance door behind her. She made sure that Aaron and Mercedes both got in their cars safely and watched them drive away.

Harper walked back to the ER. She opened the door and heard his voice. "It's going to be fine. You just need to get rid of all that nasty stuff you swallowed. I'm going to stay all night with you. You're going to feel back to your old self in the morning. Trust me. I would never lie to you." Harper did not know whether to clear her throat to let him know of her presence or continue to watch the compassion that this man had for an animal that he had just met. Harper was feeling nostalgic. Her entire life could be summed in this one moment. Rescue was love. Love was rescue. She was ready to inform Crispin she was in the room when Fred start foaming at his mouth. This was the beginning. Harper told

Crispin she would get the warm cloths to wipe his face and keep him clean. She handed him a silver pan so Crispin could catch the affect effects of the poison.

Forty-five minutes of heaving and finally, Fred had calmed down. Now to put an IV in of fluids to keep dehydration from setting in. Crispin told Harper he could do the IV and for her to clean up. Harper nodded and began throwing the towels in the bin for laundry. She got the sanitizer out and began the cleaning and wipe-down process of all beds, counters, and equipment. Harper turned and inquired if Crispin could place Fred in his recovery crate. "Absolutely," Crispin stated.

When Crispin returned, he did not see Harper. He looked to the left and then to the right. He smiled. She was laying on the cot that he assumed was for when the good doctor needed to spend the night to keep a watch on her patients. He walked over and knelt down. He lightly placed his hand on her shoulder to let her know he was there.

Harper reached for Crispin. "Thank you. I'll be staying but you can go home." "Nope. I'm going to stay. We started this together and we will finish together. So scoot over. We both need sleep."

Harper was ready to object. She should object. She should put up some kind of argument but to be honest she was exhausted. She scooted and he looked at Harper. "Close your eyes, Harper. I can hear him. I turned on the monitors." Her eyebrows puckered. He pointed to the top counters. "Instinct from being a pediatrician."

Harper turned her back to him. He met her back with his. Both shared the pillow and pulled up the covers to their waist. Fred would be fine. Crispin was sure.

CHAPTER 14

Something was blocking her. Something was prohibiting her freedom. Why could Harper not roll over. There was also something heavy laying across her waist. She took her free hand and wiped her face. Where was she? Better yet, who was with her? She tried to shift and when she did, he pulled her tighter to his chest. The feel of the hot skin of his chest against hers was enough to send her over the edge. And, good lawd, was he even wearing pants?

Before Harper could devise a plan as to how to wake Dr. Crispin Steele, he whispered softly on her ear "Keep shifting like you are, and I can promise danger only awaits you. It's your call." Oh great, now he was awake because of her. And no matter, she would have to climb over him to achieve freedom.

"Fine, I'll lay here as stiff as a board," Harper pouted. Crispin chuckled. He knew he had her where she was most vulnerable – in his arms. Had he planned to wake up this morning being extremely aroused? No. He had only known Harper for a mere 38 hours. Well, no, that wasn't the truth. He had known her for approximately two weeks, if you went back to the date she rescued him.

Crispin placed his hand on her waist to position her body so they were facing each other. "What, what do you want, Dr. Steele? Harper questioned him. "This is what I want." Before she could respond, Crispin leaned in and nibbled Harper's bottom lip. He broke away to trail kisses down the side of Harper's neck. Why? Why was he doing this? To test Harper's will power. Right now, Harper had none. The kisses were with purpose. The suckling of Harper's lower lip was with intent. Crispin pulled back to look at Harper. "Harper, if I go any further, I cannot stop. Do you understand what I am saying?" Harper nodded. She could not speak. If Crispin could read her mind, he would know the truth. She did not want him to stop.

"Look at me, Harper. Give me your hand." Harper placed her hand in Crispin's. He then lightly position her hand over his manhood. Harper could feel the desire. Crispin placed his hand on top of hers. "Trust me, don't be afraid," he whispered. Harper smiled. "It's you who should be afraid, Dr. Steele." She began to massage Crispin. Crispin took a breath. "Am I doing it right?" Was she doing it right? Who was this woman? Was she a vixen in disguise? "Who are you, Dr. Harper Steele?" Crispin smiled and rolled Harper on her back. He nudged himself between Harper. She would need to spread her legs to accommodate him. Harper was still holding Crispin. "You can let go, Harper. Can you feel me? Can you feel my need?" "All of a sudden, Harper could not talk. She was playing with fire and she knew it. She nodded her head. "Open your legs just a bit more." When she did, Crispin began the movement in and out. Even though both had clothes on, it was becoming a heated situation. Harper did not remember turning the heat on. She was burning from the inside out. Crispin sat up and pulled Harper with him. "We don't need this" and he lifted her hands over her head and removed her scrub top and shirt. Harper watched as Crispin laid it on the floor. He then took his scrub top off. Harper inhaled deeply. Crispin was muscular. His arms, which had just been holding her, were ripped. She did not want to tell him, but good lawd, he oozed sex. Underneath the façade of being a pediatrician, Crispin was not just hot, he was smoking hot.

Harper forget she was laying beneath this doctor. A doctor whom she had only known for less than 38 hours but technically, approximately two weeks, if you counted his rescue. Crispin pulled one strap of her bra off her shoulder. This gave him easy access to place small dotted kisses on the shoulder until he reached the side of her neck and felt her arch. He then moved to her earlobe and began suckling at the bottom and moving around her lobe with his tongue.

Harper instinctively arched into Crispin. With his other hand, he rubbed his thumb near her bellybutton, just enough to elicit a moan. He then moved to her back and began to pull her scrub pants down. He began trailing kisses down Harper's side. As he kissed, he maneuvered his way towards the most intimate of spots. Harper felt as if she had left her body and could only watch what was taking place in slow motion. She did not realize where the kisses were beginning and ending. All she knew was that Crispin was bringing thoughts to her mind that could only manifest into trouble (for both of them). Harper's body was betraying her. Inch by inch, Crispin had revealed her vulnerability. Crispin knew that just a few more kisses and the scrubs would be where he needed them. Away from her body. As he took both his hands and uncovered the delicate flower he needed to taste, he looked up at Harper. Her eyes were dark with desire. Her lips were swollen with desire. Her legs had opened unknowingly. Yes, Crispin would have her and he would have all of her. "Harper, once these scrubs are completely removed from blocking what I so desperately crave, there is no turning back. I need to be inside of you." Harper could not speak. The words would not come. She could not say no because she was feeling the same way. She needed him. She needed him inside. She wanted to feel his manhood slide in. She could only nod her head yes to Crispin's question. Crispin was in awe of her body's gentle shape, her narrow shoulders exposed, her round hips and breasts enhanced.

"Good. Come here, please." Crispin reached for her and pulled her forward. As she leaned against his chest for support, he reached around Harper and like the whisper of the wind, her bralette was no more. He began to kiss Harper's neck. As she leaned back, he captured her head with one hand and began to roam with the other towards her breast. Crispin took the palm of his hand and massaged Harper's breast. He began to rub the nipple between his fingers. He felt the nipple enlarge. Harper pushed against his fingers. "Please, Crispin." "Please, Crispin what", Crispin whispered. Crispin was tempting her. Lord, she could not deny him. "Kiss me like there's no tomorrow," Harper begged. "I"ll never stop kissing you. Open your lips, Harper." She leaned forward to kiss Crispin. The feel of her soft lips against his was both infuriating and placating. The touch of her breasts with taut nipples against his chest was like the flames of burning embers. He did not want this feeling to go away.

There was no pausing. This was the brink. There was no going back. Crispin was gone. He laid Harper back against the makeshift bed of rescue and entwined his hands with hers. She was his. She was his now. Harper reached to to untie Crispin's scrub pants and pushed them down so she could see. Crispin led her hand to his manhood. "Up and down, slow, Harper". Harper did as she was instructed. Crispin moved closer as she pulled him closer to her. She positioned Crispin's manhood with her hand and with small, gentle strokes she teased the entry to heaven. Crispin inhaled. "Harper, I need to be inside of you. To feel your moistness, to feel your warmth. Wrap your legs around me and allow me in." Harper could only watch as her legs wrapped themselves around Crispin and he gently pushed his way into her clit. He did quick in and out motions to raise Harper's excitement of what was to come. He knew when she was ready. Their motions were one. Crispin stopped at the outer part and spread her clit with his finger. Yes, she was wet with desire. Harper could not take any more. She enveloped Crispin's finger and began thrusting motions. Crispin withdrew and with one thrust he was inside of Harper. Lawd, she was warm and inviting. He wanted to please Harper. He wanted to see her face when he brought her to the heights of ecstasy. "Open your eyes. Look at me, Harper." Harper did. Crispin's eyes were smoky with lust and exuded sex. With each thrust, Crispin would bring promise. Harper grabbed Crispin's butt with her hands and pulled him deeper inside. "Please, now," Harper begged. And so, Crispin released all of the energy he had held back.

He kissed Harper on the forehead, then her nose and then her lips with promises to come. "Are you okay?" For the first time in her life, Harper felt out of control. She blushed. Crispin noticed. "I am fine, Crispin. Are you okay?" "If you mean, did I enjoy myself and the outcome, yes, Harper, I did."

CHAPTER 15

Before Harper could explain herself and her moment of weakness, Harper heard the key turn the lock in the front entry. "Get up. Get dressed. Get out. Oh my lawd, they can't find you here, Crispin. What will I tell Dan and Mercedes?" "Well, the truth might be the best. Like, I just made wild, passionate love with Dr. Crispin Steele and it was the best ever. Sound good to you," Crispin began to laugh.

"Now you want to be funny. Seriously, Crispin. Move. I've got to get dressed. The office is opening." Harper shoved Crispin to the floor. Within 5 seconds she was fully dressed in again in scrubs and had her hair pulled back in a bun. She threw Crispin's scrubs at him. " You're like a turtle. Chop, chop. You can leave through the emergency exit in the back. Now, please." Harper watched as Crispin stood up. Stark naked for her to watch. Put his scrubs on. Walked towards Harper. Grabbed her around the waist and kissed her hard. "There will be more of this. Trust me." Harper shook her head no. "Not today. Not tomorrow. Not again, Dr. Steele." Crispin chuckled "Yes, there will and you know it. This discussion is for another time. See you later." "Crispin, please just leave. Before Dan and Mercedes walk in or hear us," Harper pleaded. Crispin swatted her butt. "As you command, Dr. True."

Harper made sure she could see Crispin leave. He had just walked through the ER exit, when Dan walked through the door with the exclamation of "You've been here all night. How's our patient."

Harper looked at Dan and rubbed her face with her hands. "Headed that way now. We did not encounter anything unusual during the night. Fred slept well." Dan cleared his throat. "We?" "I meant I did not encounter anything unusual. Long night, Dan." "Whatever you say, Dr. True, whatever you say."

As Dan was following Harper, he glanced to the cot and noticed a pair of boxers and socks thrown carelessly at the end. Fred was the urgent issue at the moment, but boy there was going to be some explaining to do and Dan could not wait to hear how the morning, or even better, the evening unraveled.

Fred was up. He was wagging his tail and even placed his paw through the wire crate. Oh, yes, Fred was looking good. If Fred could keep down his morning meal and was drinking regularly and handling all personal business, Harper would call Aaron to inform him to come get his beloved companion. She opened the crate doors. "Come on Mr. Fred. Let's go take a walk and see what the world looks like this morning."

The entire week at the shelter flew by fast. Had it been just five days since Harper and Crispin made love. And why was she thinking about Dr. Crispin Steele and what he was up to. Had he thought about that night? Did he feel he had made a mistake? I wonder what he has been up to this week? Why Harper cared she did not know.

It was just a few days away. The town folk knew that the shelter and rescue relied on folk who loved animals as much as Harper did to keep the shelter afloat. One of her biggest fundraisers was about to kick off. It was famous around, not just their small community, but around the surrounding counties. Several folk travelled three to four hours just to participate in the Santa Paws Christmas pageant. This was Harper's calling. She loved raising awareness about rescue. But more she loved every animal that came through the rescue. Some had been there for just a few weeks. Some had been there for more than a year. Some were frequent flyers – meaning they had been returned more than once for some reason or another. These were the sad cases. This is what made Harper fight for the dollars needed for the shelter. It was not just for the shelter, but for these fur babies that needed a voice.

CHAPTER 16

Harper was in the back office. She had to finalize confirmation of the sponsors for the Santa Paws Christmas pageant. Mercedes had informed her she was going to run and grab everyone lunch. Dan was in the back cleaning beds and doing rounds. Harper heard the Christmas bells tinkle as she knew the shelter had company. She hollered to whoever it was "I'll be right there." She inked and added the bronze sponsor to the excel spreadsheet. Things were looking good. She jumped up and jogged to the front counter. Harper stopped dead in her tracks.

It was him. It was the man she had made love to a few weeks ago on the cot in the back room while Fred was recuperating (why did this all hit her at once). "Good morning, Dr. Steele." Crispin smiled. "Is that any way to greet the man you…" 'Stop, stop right there," Harper pointed her finger at him. "Don't you dare say any more." Crispin laughed. "What, you don't want anyone to know. Or is it, you have NOT told anyone?" Harper was turning red. Lawd, he could get under her skin. Crispin did not know if she was mad or if she was blushing from the memory of that night – actually early morning love session. "Tell me you did not enjoy yourself," Crispin point blank stated. "No…I don't know. I mean, yes, I did…" Harper started the sentence and then looked at Crispin. "Never mind. Crispin, how can I help you?" Crispin walked towards Harper. "Well for starters, how about a kiss good morning?" Harper's eyes widened. He was not going to kiss her. Before she could comment with what Crispin knew was going to be a "I don't think so reply", he pulled her into his arms and kissed her on the forehead. Harper leaned into Crispin. "Was that so bad, Harper?" She dare not look at him. She could not. She had missed Crispin. She could not put her finger on it and she did not want to analyze the why. Crispin placed his finger under her chin. "Ask me, Harper." "Ask you what?" she stated innocently. "Ask me to kiss you," Crispin chuckled. "You just did, Crispin," Harper stated as a matter of fact.

The door flew open. "Are you two just going to stand there? A little help would be appreciated." Mercedes was rolling her eyes. Crispin rushed to grab the drinks that Mercedes was trying to balance in the drink holder. Harper reached for their lunch. Mercedes had seen the exchange when she burst through the door. Something was happening or had already happened. She looked at Harper. "So did you ask him? Did he say yes? You know the town is going to be all over this." Harper was ready to throttle Mercedes. She had only mentioned in passing that she may ask Dr. Crispin Steele to be one of the three celebrity judges for the Santa Paws Christmas Pageant. Now the cat was out of the bag.

Crispin looked at Mercedes and then Harper. "Well, since she did not tell me, spill the beans, Mercedes. What is taking place?" Crispin was staring at Harper. "It's the shelter's biggest fundraiser. This event brings in enough sponsors and financial support to keep us afloat and to get all the supplies needed for the upcoming year," Mercedes was rattling. Crispin could tell Mercedes was filled with such excitement about this event. He caught Harper out of the corner of his eye watching him. "Dr. True, do you need me?" Okay, he knew what he was doing. Oh yes, Dr. Steele was toying with her. Harper thought to herself. Just do it. What's the worst thing that happen? That was a loaded question but all he could was say no, right?

"Crispin, I do need you. Wipe that grin off your face. I would like to ask if you could judge our annual Santa Paws Christmas Pageant. It's our biggest and largest fundraiser for the shelter and…" "Harper, yes. I'll judge."

Mercedes jumped. "Then it's a done deal. The judges are finalized. We can announce. This is going to be the best pageant ever."

"I agree with you, Mercedes. It's going to be the best," Crispin winked at Harper. Harper could not take her eyes off Crispin. "Would you like to stay for lunch and we can go over the details." "Why not, I don't have plans until the evening." Harper should have been happy but the last words "plans until the evening" caught her off guard. Crispin watched as Harper took in the meaning of those last words. He did have plans. Plans for dinner with his mom and dad, just like he had been doing for the past two weeks. Harper didn't need to know who his plans were with.

Mercedes rushed them towards the kitchen. She and Dan would handle the front. Dan heard his name. He was always a day late and a dollar short when it came to keeping up with Mercedes and Harper and the antics of rescue.

As they walked towards the kitchen, Crispin placed his hand on the small of Harper's back. A shiver went through Harper. His touch had a warming effect. It was either that or Harper had a fever. Either way, Harper was hot underneath her office jacket and scrubs. She needed to sit apart from Crispin. He pulled the chair out and, of course, sat right next to Harper. He could have chosen the other side, but no he did not. Her emotions were on high alert with just the fact he was sitting next to her.

Harper reached for the plates, napkins and utensils. She set the table then reached for Crispin's hand. "We need to say grace." Crispin nodded. At that moment, something changed for Crispin. He watched as Harper raised her head from the finished prayer. He felt a cool whisper on his neck. Oh, definitely, changes were coming.

He wasted no time by jumping from the stove to the fire. "Harper, tell me more about this pageant and being a celebrity judge. What are my duties and responsibilities?"

"Crispin, it's nothing really. Please do not feel obligated to commit. I know you are a busy important man. Do not worry about it," Harper stated. "Can you please let me decide if I am too busy. Can you tell me about the day's timeframe, let me decide. Deal?"

Harper could tell he was like a pup with a bone. He was not going to let this go. "Fine. Our entire town comes with their pets dressed in their favorite Christmas attire. You and two other "town celebs" will judge and pick the top 5 best dressed and then you must decide a winner from the top 5. It's not that big."

Crispin listened with intensity to all that Harper was explaining. "Is that all. I'm your man. I'm your judge." Harper smiled. He seemed enthusiastic about judging and Harper knew he had NEVER judged a pageant, and especially, one with animals dressed in their best and fav Christmas attire. Harper stood up. She held her hand out. Crispin brought her hand to his lips and kissed it. Harper did not know whether to laugh. She was completely caught off guard. Harper giggled. "No, no, I meant a handshake to seal the deal." Crispin stood and swept a piece of hair from Harper's face to her ear. "I'd rather kiss you." And that is just what Dr. Crispin Steele did. He kissed Harper. Harper kissed him back and then Crispin's tongue found its way to heaven. Harper's tongue. He was teasing Harper. She inhaled and that was Crispin's opportunity to change the mood of the kiss. He pulled Harper towards him. She did not pull away. In fact, she leaned into Crispin. "Oh, Dr. Harper True, what have you done to me? Not only did you rescue me, you now have me judging a pageant." "Nothing that you did not want, Dr. Crispin Steele." "Oh, I know what I want. I know what I want right now. And I know I could have what I want." Harper placed her hands on his chest to prevent any further play. Harper knew where this could lead. Danger. Trouble. She did not have time for either.

Crispin saw her eyebrows crinkle. She was fighting what he knew was and would be inevitable should the kiss continue. He also knew she needed to stay on task. He kissed her on the tip of her nose. "We shall continue this. I promise I will remember where we left this discussion. Get to work and stop fretting. I will help you and the shelter. I will be the best judge ever." He turned and winked and was gone before she could thank him. If every time she was around Crispin and went weak at the knees at just the sight of him, this pageant would never be finished. She shook her head. "Get your head out of the clouds, Harper. There is work to do and a shelter that needs funds but especially, the fur babies needed to know they would have food, drink and a warm bed to lay on." Priorities, priorities, priorities.

CHAPTER 17

The week flew by. It was Friday. Everything had to be set up before the big Santa Paws Christmas pageant on Saturday morning. What a whirlwind day. The stage and ramp had been set up. Lighting, sound, trussing, speakers, microphones, Christmas tree, sleigh, and presents. Harper had not expected Crispin to show up on Friday afternoon at the shelter to ask what was left to be done but he surprised her. He had been surprising her in many ways since rescuing him. Dan made sure that all rescues were fed, warm bedding, business taken care of and light warmers left on. Mercedes ran out the door screaming she would meet everyone at the towne square with decorations. Harper turned and asked Crispin "ready?" "Yes mam, I'm at your disposal."

Everyone (just like previous years) worked as a team. Harper had not changed the setup of the pageant for five years. Harper and Crispin arrived. It was coming together rather nicely. Crispin walked to the stage and began taking a look at the stage. Harper did not like "that look". "Crispin, what's wrong?" "Well, what if the sleigh were moved into the corner over here and the presents placed inside instead of on the outside. What if the Christmas tree were moved to this corner? And what if we trimmed the stage in the big Christmas light bulbs with garland?" Harper could not resist. "Crispin, who are you?" Everything he had mentioned changing was not a bad idea. It would enhance the stage and bring more attention to the animals that would be competing for the coveted 14k gold water and food bowl. This was just icing on the cake for the winner. Of course, there were other prizes for all participants, as well as special sponsorship packages for the top 5, which included the winner. Harper had this event down to the precise minute.

Crispin tilted his head. "Too much?" Harper couldn't contain her smile. "No. It's just right." The evening finished with all in agreement that the decorations and stage were phenomenal. Harper applauded to capture Dan, Mercedes and Crispin's attention. "This is it. Tomorrow we will host and produce the largest fundraiser for the shelter. You guys know what is riding on this. Supplies of food, pads, medications, beds and potential fosters and adoptions. Rescue does not stop. It is 24/7 – 365. There is not a second that goes by that some fur baby does not need to be rescued. They are counting on us. I'm counting on you." Before she could stop it, a tear formed and Harper began to cry. Her entire world was this shelter/rescue. Every time that Harper travelled in the middle of the night for rescue, her heart would beat so fast as if it was going to explode from her chest. Once the rescue(s) was in her arms, Harper knew the first few hours were crucial. Most of the animals were mistrusting and a bit aggressive with her. If only, love could be given freely. If only, love were unconditional. If only. Crispin made a move towards her and she looked up. She had been in her own world. "Hey, come here. I have something for you." Harper made a face. Her lips curled in a smirk. "Of course, you do." "Why do you think I always want to get in your scrubs, Dr. Harper True." Harper busted out laughing. "Because you do." "Guilty," Crispin admitted. "But not tonight. Let's get you home so we are prepared for tomorrow." Harper nodded. She mouthed the words "thank you." "Any time, Dr. True."

Harper woke bright and early. Before the alarm went off, which was unusual. She typically hit snooze at least two, may be three times, if she was really tired. She smiled. This day was going to be flipping awesome. She showered. Hair up in a knotty bun. Jeans, thermal long sleeve tee, boots and her favorite puppy and kitten scarf – she was ready.

Crispin hollered at his mom. "Can't eat breakfast. Judging a pageant. You guys should come. It starts at noon." That was as much information as he had time to relay. Crispin hated to admit it. He was a bit nervous. The rescue, the animals, the dollars raised, judging and Harper. He felt his entire world had been turned inside out. He knew he could not be late. There was a special introduction of the judges.

Harper parked at the shelter. The walk was not long to where the pageant would be held. She just wanted to check on the rescue and to make sure that all was well. She unlocked the entry door. She heard him. Dan was singing to the rescues. At the top of his lungs. Harper backed out slowly so he did not realize that she had been there. She should have known that Dan would be there for the morning routine. Harper was truly blessed by Dan and his love of the shelter but more his passion for rescue.

She locked the door to the rescue. She looked to the beautiful sun rising and whispered "I just don't need you. They do too." She closed her eyes and whispered "Amen." Harper was hoping against hope that she would have at least 15 participants for the pageant. This would be an addition of three more than last year. Harper stopped. There was a bunch of barking and laughing and "how ya doing this fine morning". No. There was no way. She peeked around the building. She did not want to get her hopes up. She stepped forward and there they were. The check in table for participants to register was backed up. Mercedes waved her hand in the air, in a sweeping motion. Was she saying hello? No. She had a panic look on her face. "Harper. Get over here. There's no time to tell you good morning. Come on. We need to get everyone their contestant number." Harper made her way through the crowd. Wishing everyone a good morning. Thanking each one for coming. Rubbing the heads of pets as she passed by. She sat down behind the table and shouted "next". By the time, she and Mercedes were finished with registration and numbers had been handed to everyone, the total count of contestants was over sixty-three (63). Harper was overjoyed. Just with the entry fees, six months were going to be covered of medications for all the shelter residents.

Harper stood up and found Mr. Gabe, the town's mayor. He was a loveable kinda guy. He had adopted a senior basset hound from the shelter that no one wanted because of his age but Mr. Gabe told her that age was just a number and that Max was wiser than the rest of the animals because of his maturity. In truth, Mr. Gabe reminded Harper of the singer, Burl Ives. He had that personality and demeanor that just in his presence, you felt the Christmas spirit. He tapped his watch, which could only mean time to get the show on the road or on the stage. Harper acknowledged the tapping. Before she could take the stage, a hand slid around her waist. He pulled her close to his chest. He whispered behind her ear. "Look. Look at what you have done. All these people have brought their animals because of how you have touched their lives with rescue." She leaned back for him to easier access. "I'm so proud of you, Harper. Take that stage and show them who you are."

Harper nodded. As she stepped away, he squeezed her hand as a quiet show of support. Mr. Gabe reached for her hand to help her walk the steps up the stage, where he had been waiting, he told her for fifteen minutes. Now, she knew that was not true. But she knew he did not like to start anything late. There was a time frame to follow. Harper took the mic and the applause began. She began the introduction of Mr. Gabe. He was beaming from ear to ear. He welcomed the town to the Santa Paws Christmas pageant. He then called for the judges, one by one, to come to the stage. When it came time for Crispin, several women in the audience were not just hollering, but whistling. Harper felt an emotion she had not felt for a very long time. Jealousy. She knew that she and Crispin were not a "thing" but yet, neither were these other women who just happened to be Harper's friends.

Before Harper could mull over this feeling, the judges had taken their seat and the steps had been replaced by a ramp for the animals to walk up for their time to shine. One by one, the contestants took their call. There were four Xs on the stage for the owners to be sure to use as a guidance so that everyone could see the pet / contestant. There was such a plethora of diversification with the contestants, ranging from bunnies, chickens, roosters, pot belly piggies, big piggies, miniature horses, cats, dogs, guinea pigs, and one ferret.

Mr. Gabe introduced each participant. He read a bio on each one. Their name, their momma and daddy's name, their favorite hobby, their favorite food and their favorite Christmas song. All was shared with the audience while walking the stage in there outfits.

If he were honest with himself, Crispin could admit he did not think he would enjoy judging, but he was wrong. He loved it. He loved seeing the animals competing and their Christmas attire, especially, the ones with the crinoline skirts. There were Santa Clauses, there were angels, there were elves but there was one that just took Crispin's heart. It was Rocky, the bulldog. He was a Victorian bulldog. Crispin knew this because the English bulldog was the smaller of the breed in height, weight and stature. Rocky was dressed as a Christmas donut. Sitting atop his head were the antenna sprinkles. On each side of Rocky's body was the circular shape of a glazed donut. Rocky was wearing a big beautiful, colorful bow tie with audience while sprinkle colors. The donut had sprinkles attached to each side. As Rocky made his way to the stage, Crispin could not stop smiling. His owner was a stout man. Crispin could tell how much Rocky was loved. He knew this because of how the owner was bending down talking to him and giving Rocky kisses. Rocky was giving paw high fives. As Rocky hit each X marked on the stage, he performed a special task. He waved to the audience with one paw. He turned in a circle so the town folk could see both sides of the sprinkled donut. He then smiled to where you could see his teefers. The last X was where the town folk were clapping and cheering loudly. Rocky stopped and sat up on his hind legs and rubbed his paws together as if clapping with the community. This breed was loyal. The memories of Gertie came rushing back.

From the corner of the stage, Harper watched all of the entries as they entered and exited the stage. The pageant was running on time and those in attendance were having such a great time rooting for their favorite. Harper made sure that Mercedes and Dan were picking up the scoresheets and tallying so there was no delay in the announcement of the winners. As she turned to approach Mercedes to see how the tally was coming, she saw Crispin. He looked lost in thought. Had something happened at the judges' table? Was he not feeling well? Harper approached the table. Took the scoresheets up and looked at Crispin "Everything ok, Dr. Steele?" "I'm okay, Harper. Just reminiscing over the love of my life." Harper did not know what to say. She had never heard Crispin speak of a 'significant other'. Of course, she had never asked if he were romantically involved with anyone. This was not the time nor the place to broach this subject. She nodded and stepped away from the table.

CHAPTER 18

The scores were tallied and completed. The announcement was ready. Harper gave the nod to Mayor Gabe. He walked the steps. The town folk could feel the anticipation in the air. Who would be crowned the King or Queen of Santa Paws Christmas pageant. Mr. Gabe cleared his throat. "Ladies and Gentlemen, we have the results. This envelope contains our top 5. I will begin with the fourth runner up, third runner up, second runner up, first runner up and our winner. Thank you to everyone who participated in the Santa Paws Christmas pageant. Dr. Harper True and staff could not keep the shelter going were it not for folk like you and your generous donations to the shelter as well as your participation in the pageant. With our generous sponsors and donations and the registration fees, I am excited to announce that the shelter has raised over $75,000. I hope you realize what has been accomplished. Medications, supplies, and bedding will be readily available for the coming year for the intake of new rescues. Thank you."

Here we go. As I call your name, please take the stage. Please stay on stage for those photo ops. Dr. True will place you where she needs you. Our fourth runner up is Herbert, the pig. Mr. Gabe waited until Herbert had been placed on stage. Our third runner up is Jezebel, the bunny. Harper guided Jezebel and her owner to the opposite side of Herbert. Our second runner up is Action Jackson, the cat. Harper watched as Action Jackson took the stage. Harper knew to keep a bit of distance between Action Jackson and Jezebel. "We are almost there ladies and gentlemen. One more to go and then the winner." Please welcome to the stage our first runner up, Livvie, the basset hound. The crowd roared. Harper could not help but laugh. There was no way Livvie was going to walk back up the ramp to take the stage. Harper watched as Ginny, Livvie's owner, picked her up and positioned Livvie over both her arms. Harper escorted them to where they needed to stand. She smiled at her best friend. "Congrats, honey."

"And now a drum roll please. This is the moment you have been waiting for. Dr. Harper True and Endless Pawsabilities Rescue are proud to announce your new winner of the Santa Paws Christmas pageant. Please give it up for Rocky, the Victorian bulldog. Crispin heard the loudest scream of exuberance. Crispin watched as Rocky's owner ran up the steps with Rocky right on his heels. Both stopped right in front of Mayor Gabe. Mercedes walked forward to place the crown on Rocky's head and then to drape the red velvet Christmas cape across the donut costume and Rocky's shoulders. Harper could have sworn that Rocky was cheesing for the audience. She positioned the runner ups and Rocky, based on their placement. Mayor Gabe thanked the judges and thanked the town again. The local newspaper was taking pics as quick as they could. There was only a certain window of time that all the animals would sit still.

Harper left the stage. She needed to find Crispin and thank him. She needed to thank the other judges, as well, but Crispin was her first priority. She saw him trying to sneak out. Harper did not know why. Something in her gut told her to stop Crispin from leaving. Harper jumped into action and ran towards Crispin. She was out of breath when she reached him. She held her hand in the air to capture his attention and hollered "Don't you dare leave." Crispin heard Harper. His emotions were raw. Seeing Rocky had made him long for what would never be again. When Gertie had passed, Crispin did not want to get another dog. It felt as if he were betraying Gertie and there was no replacing Gertie.

"Crispin, stop! Don't make me run after you!" Crispin turned to face Harper. "Out of shape, Dr. True?" Harper put her hands on her hip. "Nope. I want to thank you for judging. I also want to know why you are leaving?" She pleaded with Crispin. "What's wrong?" "Oh, Harper, if I told you, you wouldn't feel the same about me. You would just call me sentimental." Harper said "try me."

And so Crispin began the story of his rescue. His very first rescue. His first love – Gertie. He bared his soul to Harper. He did not care. Seeing Rocky had brought a yearning back that Crispin had not felt for a long time. The need for another pet. When he lost Gertie, he did not know if he would ever want to rescue, foster or adopt again. But tonight, that all changed. He saw how Rocky interacted with his owner. He missed those sloppy kisses. He missed having hair all over his coat or his scrubs and running the lint brush at least 50,000 times before leaving for the children's hospital. The memories he had kept hidden away. Harper listened to the story of Gertie. She was humbled that Crispin would share these special memories with her.

As Crispin was talking, Harper had steered them back to the shelter. She needed to do one last minute check on the rescue. "Walk with me, Crispin. Just a quick check on the fur babies." Crispin followed Harper's lead. They walked through the shelter doors. Walked down the corridor and peeked in on the rescues. All were sound asleep. Several were snoring louder than a chainsaw. Harper reached for Crispin's hand. "Come back to my home for some hot chocolate." Crispin began to rub the inside of Harper's hand. "Look, Harper, if I come back to your home, I am not coming for hot chocolate. You know it and I know it. Do you still want me to come to your home for hot chocolate?" Harper knew what that underlying statement meant. Hot chocolate was not going to be the main topic for the evening. She blushed. "I know."

Crispin squeezed her hand. "I'll follow you, Harper. My rental car is parked over here behind the shelter." Harper laughed nervously. "Mine, too". As Harper pulled into her driveway, she turned the truck off. She watched as Crispin's headlights shadowed her truck. The lights turned off and Crispin got out. She could hear his footsteps approach her driver's side door. She was holding on to the steering wheel. In reality, she was gripping the steering wheel. Harper knew when she opened the door, there was no turning back. She did not have to make that decision. Crispin opened the door for her. "Everything okay. Doubts?" For the first time in a long time, Harper knew exactly what she wanted. She wanted Dr. Crispin Steele. In the morning, she would think of her actions but for now, tonight, she did not want to over analyze any decisions. As a doctor, she had done this all her life. Everything was precise. Everything was planned.

"No, Crispin. I have no doubts. You ready for that hot chocolate?" Harper winked. Crispin grinned. "Lead the way."

CHAPTER 19

Harper unlocked the front door. Crispin waited until Harper turned the lights on inside and held her hand out. "Welcome, Dr. Steele, to my humble abode." Crispin knew this was how her home would be. It looked as if Christmas had thrown up everywhere. There was nothing but Christmas plaid decorations. It was if he had walked into a Cracker Barrel gift shop. All the décor was themed and matched right down to the bows on the wooden staircase. The presents under the Christmas tree were even wrapped in plaid paper. "Do you like?" Harper asked Crispin. "It's you, Harper. It's all the love and feels for Christmas. Come here." Crispin pulled her into his arms. Harper hugged Crispin. This felt right. This was right. This was where she needed to be. She placed her head on his chest. Harper could feel his heart beating. Crispin kissed the top of Harper's head. "Harper, congrats on a successful fundraiser. I am so proud of you." Harper raised her head and looked Crispin square in the eyes. "Thank you. You have no idea how much that meant to me."

Crispin tipped her chin and rubbed her lips with his thumb. "Those pouty lips. I need to taste them, Harper. I need you. All of you." Harper could not answer. She nodded. "Say it, Harper. Say you need me as much as I need you." "I do."

That was all that Crispin needed. He kissed Harper. He kissed her hard. "Lips are meant to be kissed, Harper. I could kiss your lips for hours. I love the feeling of your mouth on mine. I love when you play with my tongue. I love you." Did Harper hear what she thought she had heard? Did Dr. Crispin Steele tell Dr. Harper True "I love you." Harper did not want to question the exact words. She kissed Crispin back. "Kiss me a lot, Crispin, everywhere." "Everywhere, Harper?" "Yes, everywhere," Harper whispered.

"Then come here, Dr. True." Harper did as Crispin requested. "Lift your arms, Harper." Crispin placed his hands at the bottom of the thermal tee and began to raise over Harper's head. As he was pulling the tee away from Harper, he noticed the beautiful gray lace bra she was wearing. He also was aware that Harper's breathing had increased. The rise and fall of her breasts was noticeable to the naked eye. He leaned down and kissed Harper's exposed breast. The way the pulse throbbed in Harper's neck, when he kissed it, fed Crispin's desire. He wanted Harper naked beneath him.

Crispin placed the thermal tee on the couch. He slid his hands around Harper and unsnapped her bra. Like the whisper of the wind on the ocean, he guided the bra down her arms. Harper placed her arms across her breasts. "Don't," Crispin told her. He pulled her arms away. He reached to bring her close again. Crispin began kissing her lips while one hand fumbled with the buttons on her jeans. He slid her jeans down. He placed one hand on her backside and cupped her cheek. Massaging in soft strokes, a slight whimper escaped Harper. With his other hand free, he lay his finger where desire began. "Open your legs to me, Harper." Crispin began a swirling motion near Harper's pubic hair line. Harper arched her back. Crispin kissed the side of her neck.

He slid his finger inside of Harper. She was moist to his caresses. She was warm to his touch. In and out, all the while continuing to kiss her.

This was insanity. He was teasing her. Harper wanted more. As the strokes became more quick, Harper bit her lip. She was frozen in time. Crispin picked her up without warning. "Where is your bedroom?" Harper could not answer. She pointed to where she knew he was going to take her. Crispin stopped in the doorway. "Let's get you completely out of those jeans and shoes." Crispin lay her down on the bed. He untied and then removed her lace shoe boots. The jeans were off within seconds. She lay nude on the bed.

Crispin unbuttoned his dress shirt. He then unbuckled his pants. He pitched his clothing to the side of Harper's bed. He leaned into Harper with his body. She exuded sensuality. Crispin gently flipped Harper on her side and pulled her into him. Harper could feel him. He began to tease Harper with light strokes of his finger from behind until he placed his manhood inside of Harper. She did not realize what this effect would have on her but she did not want Crispin to stop. Small strokes that were slow and then fast. Crispin nibbled on Harper's ear. He nuzzled the side of her neck. He reached his arm around to fondle the nipple of Harper's breast. Her nipple was between Crispin's thumb and finger. He was making circular motions. Harper was aching for him.

"Please, Crispin," she breathed heavily. "Please what, Harper?" Harper inhaled and shifted her body. "You know what. Please let me feel all of you." Crispin thrust inside of Harper. With slow in and out motions, he allowed her body to accommodate him. Harper's body began to match Crispin's. He followed the curve of Harper's hips with his hands.

Harper pleaded. "Now, Christian." Crispin released himself into her. Harper knew this time was different than the first. Crispin pulled her gently into his chest. He did not remove his arm. Harper was wrapped safely in the aftermath of love. "Go to sleep, Harper. I'm not going anywhere." Harper closed her eyes. She thought sleep would elude her. It did not. She placed her hand over Crispin's. She did not want to think about anything else tonight. She felt his kiss goodnight. For this moment, all was right with the world.

CHAPTER 20

Crispin woke before Harper. He took his time watching her sleep. They had not moved from each other's arms. He had never slept more peacefully. Then he remembered what he had said. He had not given her time to respond. He wondered if she would bring it up. He had never told any other woman those words. He could not put his finger on it but she was not like the rest. She was independent, intelligent and knew exactly what she wanted and how to get it done. He admired her commitment to the rescue shelter and so many that depended on her, including the rescues.

Crispin rose quietly. He did not want to wake Harper. She needed to rest after the success of the fundraiser. He ventured into the kitchen. Checking in the frig to see what he could whip up for breakfast. He found the pancake mix, the syrup and fresh strawberries. Crispin was opening several doors when he heard "Can I help you?" He turned and there she was in thermal long sleeve tee and sweats. Crispin could see that there was a bit of chill in the air. He could see her nipples taut against the tee.

"If you want, I could use the help." "First off, what are you fixing? What if I don't like it? Harper teased him. "Oh, you will like it. I'm not a bad cook," Crispin smiled. "I'll be the judge of that," Harper chuckled. As they sat at the table eating, Crispin watched as Harper took a bite and a small dribble of syrup remained on the corner of her lip. Without even warning or thinking about his action, he leaned into Harper and kissed the syrup away. And for extra points, he tugged at her bottom lip to get the remaining taste. Harper was about to ask what in the world was going on, when she saw Crispin's cell phone vibrate on the kitchen table. Crispin saw it as well. It was not his mom or dad and the only other folk it could be is the children's hospital. Crispin had told them only to call if it were an emergency.

He looked at Harper. "I have to take it, Harper, it's the children's hospital." Harper nodded she understood. Crispin walked into the den with a "Hello, this is Dr. Steele." Harper could hear bits and pieces of the conversation. There was no mistake with the last words she heard. "I'll be there as soon as I can."

Harper began to clean the kitchen table and load the dishwasher. She did not want Crispin to think she had been eavesdropping when she had been. She twisted her head towards the sound of his footsteps entering. "Everything okay?"

"No. I've got to head back sooner than anticipated. I've got to pack and leave tonight." Harper knew this day was coming. Crispin had never made any statements about how long he would be staying or when he would be leaving after his recuperation. Why did it feel as if her heart had stopped beating? She did not think it would affect her the way it was. She watched as Crispin came closer.

"I've got to leave, Harper. I have to head to my parents. Make flight arrangements. Tell them goodbye and get back to the hospital." Crispin walked to her bedroom and emerged fully dressed. "Thank you, Harper.

Harper was being thanked for ……what was he thanking her for? For making love with him, for helping with breakfast? Crispin noticed she had placed her hands on hips. This was not good. Any time a woman placed her hands on her hips, the outcome would not be in favor of the guy. This was a dead giveaway. "Harper, I wished I had more time but…." Harper held her hand up. "Don't worry. It's all good. I understand." Crispin knew that was a lie. He hadn't even had a chance to tell her why or for whom he was leaving. "Really, it's okay. I'm going to take a shower. I've cleaned the kitchen. Just let yourself out. Safe travels, Dr. Steele." Harper placed the t-towel on the sink and did not even look at Crispin as she walked passed him and into her bathroom and started the shower.

Crispin wished he could go into the details of why he was leaving so abruptly but he could not. He walked towards the door. He was leaving. He was leaving the woman who had rescued him. He was leaving the woman he was in love with.

He grabbed the door knob. Turned the lock. Closed the door behind him. One last look. Would he ever see Dr. Harper True again? He could not think about it. Time was not on his side.

CHAPTER 21

Crispin had called his mom and dad while on the road. He would need them to take him to the airport and then return the rental. Crispin would handle all the insurance paperwork from his home. Sitting on the airplane, Crispin could not help but think back to all that had happened. From the wreck to the last day with Harper. He had never laughed so much as he had done these past few weeks. What would life be like when he returned to the children's hospital? They would never believe all that he had encountered. Crispin was not the same man. He had changed. He had changed because of her.

Harper woke up Monday morning. Weekends were never long enough. Plus two times a month, the rescue was open on Saturdays til noon. Harper had spoken to Dan and Mercedes about extending the hours Monday through Friday so all could have the weekend for family and relaxation time. They just had not had the time to implement the new time frame. Harper knew most of her families would freak but then again, change was good, right? She walked to the kitchen and began the preparation for hot tea and a bagel. Here lately she had not been hungry. She had lost a bit of weight but she could attribute that to more rescues coming in and time required to take care of their needs. She thought of him. Mercedes, Dan and Ginny had asked about him. She told them she did not know. If she were honest with herself, she did want to know. She wanted to know if he thought about her? If he had walked to the phone to dial the shelter's number? If he even cared how she or the staff were doing. But then again, she knew. He didn't care. There had been nothing. Not a peep.

Harper scarfed the bagel down and burnt her tongue drinking the hot tea too quickly. She was running late. Mercedes would have her hide. The first appointment was earlier than opening. The ole hound dog, Ace, just couldn't take being around other animals. Harper knew he needed to be in the waiting room by himself and so special accommodations were made. She grabbed her backpack and locked the front door. Walked to the truck and before leaving the driveway, for a brief second, she wondered what he was doing.

Mondays were like the weekends. The overflow of patients that were still with Lullaby Children's Hospital seemed as if they were multiplying in numbers and doing so with rapid speed. As soon as Crispin would finish follow up with one, the nurse would tell him that another child needed updates with medications. Crispin was on a merry go round. He had stayed at the children's hospital from Friday night into Monday morning. Because of the time of year, the germs and love were being spread. Strep throat, pneumonia, flu, sinus infection, and then the pesky fever that would not break or lower down – everything that little ones would get because of not washing their hands and not covering their mouths when sneezing or coughing.

He finished his rounds for the morning and went to the cafeteria to grab a quick sandwich. He took the steps. He did not want to be on the elevator with staff to discuss the holidays. Christmas was just two days away. Crispin's mom had told him not to be late. The festivities and meal would start on Christmas Eve. His mom always went to the extreme, even if it were just them three or a thousand. He loved the fact that his mom paid attention to such detail. If he wanted to, he had to admit he did want to return and again he was a bit cautious. He had not called her. Oh, he had wanted to. But there was never that opportunity to call and ask how were things going. He doubted she would readily answer her phone, if she knew it were him. He had not left on good terms. He needed to remedy the situation. He wondered what she was doing.

CHAPTER 22

Friday, this was the day that everyone lived for. The day had started out with routine and then it was like a confetti gun went off. Telephone calls coming for emergency visit and the phone call that set all into panic. Ginny had called the shelter to tell Mercedes that a 911 call had been received. A young woman was in tears explaining that she had seen a box being pitched from a truck to the ditch. The young woman waited for the truck to pass and then pulled to the shoulder. She stepped cautiously toward the box and then heard the whimper. It was an animal. She opened the box with care. When she peered in, the young woman saw that it was a female dog (she was unsure of the breed) that was rather large in size. The dog's eyes were big and wide. She calmed the bulldog with her voice. The bulldog then placed her paw in the young woman's hand. She picked her up and as she did, she felt the dog's belly wiggle. This dog was not large. This dog was going to be a momma. And that's when the young lady made the call to 911. Harper could only wonder why this would happen and continued to happen. There was no explaining humans and their train of thought when it came to pets.

Harper told Mercedes she was on her way to the meet the young lady and to retrieve the little momma and bring her back for examination. "If I'm not back by 7 p.m., go ahead and close up shop. If I need you, I'll call. Otherwise, we will see how if she has suffered any injuries from the throw and talk to the young lady who witnessed the horrific incident."

From the location of the 911 call, it was about an hour drive. Harper and the young lady had agreed to meet at a local restaurant. Harper felt that was safe for all concerned.

The drive was cold. Harper could not get the heat high enough to keep her warm. Light flurries had begun to fall. Good lawd, she did not need the weather impeding the rescue. Just a few more miles and Harper would arrive to transport the precious momma back to the shelter.

Crispin could not believe his luck. He was leaving the children's hospital on time. He had packed and placed his clothing and Christmas gifts in his truck for the return home for the Christmas holidays. He hated to admit, but he was looking forward to Christmas. He had purchased a gift for her. He didn't know if she would accept it or not but he had to try. He would stop by the shelter to see if she were still working. If not, he would return again and again. He was going to see her.

Harper had told the young lady she would transport the rescue back to her shelter. The young lady was insistent that she would be following Harper back to the rescue. Harper knew that look. This young lady was decisive and did not let anyone or anything stand in her way. Harper liked her immediately. After a quick examination of the animal, Harper realized it was a momma bulldog. She was breathing heavy but then again this breed had weird noises always coming from their noses. Harper needed the momma bulldog to be relaxed as possible. One thing for certain, an x-ray would need to be done to see how many babies would be expected.

Harper pulled up to the shelter first. Good, the lights were still on, which meant Dan and Mercedes were still inside. Harper honked the horn three times which was the shelter's signal that a rescue had just arrived and all hands were on deck. Mercedes threw open the door. Dan had the medical cart ready and warm and all went into motion. The young lady was standing and watching. Harper asked her to have a seat. They would get the momma bulldog cleaned and examined and come get her. She nodded her head. Harper saw a tear trickle down her cheek. "Don't worry, she's going to be okay. We just need to see how far along she is." The young lady agreed.

Harper watched as Dan got the bowl of warm water to begin cleaning the momma. All the while, singing Christmas songs. Mercedes had already pulled the x-ray machine close. It would take less than 10 seconds to find out how many precious babies she was carrying.

The front office door bell rang. Someone else had entered the shelter. All three looked at each other and said "I thought you locked the front door." Mercedes told them she would check it out. Harper and Dan began the examination. The x-ray had been done. The momma bulldog had cooperated with no fuss. Dan smiled. They had counted 5 babies. All were doing well from what the x-rays revealed. Now to inform the young lady who had rescued the momma bulldog. Harper had just placed her hand on the doorknob to open it when Mercedes burst through. "You got a visitor." Harper looked at Mercedes with raised eyebrows. "Is it another patient or another rescue, Mercedes?" "Well, depends on how you look at him. He's a bit different than most of our patients or rescues. He has two legs and is standing upright." Harper was too tired to do all this guessing. "I'll take care of him." Harper was tired. She was whooped. Her sweats and bed were calling her name. She walked through the shelter hallway and opened the door to the front main entry. She had started to tell the young lady how the momma bulldog was doing when she heard his voice.

"Harper, can I help with anything?" She turned to look at him and before she could stop herself, she began with "What, you want to help me now? Two weeks have gone by. I've not heard hide nor hair from you." Crispin knew she was ticked. Her cheeks were flushed. Before she could say another word, Crispin grabbed her and kissed her hard. "I've missed you. Have you missed me?" "You're serious right now. What do you think. You whispered those three words to me and then you leave. Dr. Crispin Steele, why are you here"? "I did not want to kiss you goodbye again. I want to kiss you in the morning and for all mornings and nights. I did not want any misunderstandings as to my intentions and I think there may have been from the confused look on your face. Why not show up in person and tell you?"

Before she could respond, Crispin touched the side of Harper's face. "Tell me, Dr. Harper True, that you do not feel the same way and I'll turn around." Harper shook her head. "I do, Crispin. I love you without the why, the how or the where. I love you simply because it is what it is. I cannot explain it. Love can not be explained."

Crispin smiled. "Come here, Harper." Harper walked toward Crispin. "One more time and for good measure – I am in love with you, Harper True."

Before Harper could respond, there was a noise. The sound of someone clearing their throat with an apologetic "I'm so sorry, but I'll take her."

Harper and Crispin had overlooked the fact that the young lady who had called the shelter to rescue the momma bulldog had been and was still standing in the front lobby with Harper and Crispin.

All began to laugh. Harper smiled and winked. "We did not forget about you. Let's begin the paperwork and get you confirmed as the foster mom. Just out of curiosity, what's your name?" Harper asked.

"Hope. My name is Hope." Crispin squeezed Harper's hand. "Of course, it would be Hope."

The story of rescue…the story of love…the story of FURever!!!

Kentucky Romance Author

The Day You Go from Romance Junkie to
 # 1 Best Selling Romance Author

de de began pursuing her dream of becoming a romance author at the age of 30. Born and raised on the farm in Rooster Run, KY, de de was raised on the core values of the 3Cs (kindness, caring and compassion). Throughout her young adulthood, de de volunteered in the community with her family, and specifically, her grandmother, Bea. Growing up in the country, romance novels were the escape to another world. de de knew that one day her dream of writing a romance novel would come to fruition. Fast forward to 2018, when de de picked the book back up that she had begun in her early 30s. As in life, circumstances and direction change the course BUT never the ending goal. Learning the industry and working with her publisher, Beyond Global Publishing, God opened many doors and many connects and de de has never looked back.

de de has had the opportunity and blessing to work with and meet the best screenwriters, producers, directors in the film industry during The Story Summit cruise (Randal Kleiser of Grease and Rosa Salazar Arenas, screenwriter of over 6,000 hours of prime time television). The next step is to take the book series to screenwrite, movie, song and video.

de de became a published Kentucky romance author in 2018. She is the #1 best-selling romance author of the Two Degrees Series, which features her son, Bo, as the male model. Little did de de know that her child would become the next FabiBo.

de de has served as a board member of The Dream Factory of Louisville, KY, Opal's Dream Foundation, Spalding University – Athletic Board. de de received the coveted 2018 WLKY Bell Award for her volunteerism within her community.

de de is active within the pageant industry. She is the co-preliminary director of the Miss My Old Kentucky Home (a prelim to the state /national of the Miss America system). She is the co-director in 3 festival prelims (the Hillview Festival, the Bullitt Blast festival and the Buttermilk festival).

FAMILY (family always mean I love you) and this is true in de de's life. So many kind hearted folk have travelled the journey. de de encourages others to live by HIS word – Acts 20:35. She has been married 35+ years to her best friend (Scott) from high school. She has two sons and 3 rescued fur babies.

www.ingramcontent.com/pod-product-compliance
Lightning Source LLC
LaVergne TN
LVHW020428080526
838202LV00055B/5082